THE FEATHERED SERPENT

Edgar Wallace started his career in Fleet Street selling newspapers when he was eleven years old. He went on to become one of the most prolific and popular authors of his generation, earning and losing millions of pounds. He wrote 175 novels, 24 plays, and there have been 160 films made based on his novels, more than any other author. He died in Hollywood in 1932 while working on the screenplay for *King Kong*.

Edgar Wallace

THE
FEATHERED
SERPENT

HODDER

A CIP catalogue record for this title is available from the British Library

ISBN 978 0 340 92286 6

Typeset in Sabon by Hewer Text UK Ltd, Edinburgh
Printed and bound by Mackays of Chatham Ltd, Chatham, Kent

Hodder Headline's policy is to use papers that are natural, renewable
and recyclable products and made from wood grown in sustainable forests.
The logging and manufacturing processes are expected to conform
to the environmental regulations of the country of origin.

Hodder & Stoughton Ltd
A division of Hodder Headline
338 Euston Road
London NW1 3BH

To Daphne du Maurier

I

What annoyed Peter Dewin most, as it would have annoyed any properly constituted reporter, was what he called the mystery-novel element in the Lane case.

A real good crime story may gain in value from a touch of the bizarre, but all good newspaper men stop and shiver at the mention of murder gangs and secret societies, because such things do not belong to honest reporting, but are the inventions of writers of best or worst sellers.

Did not McCarthy of the *Star* drop the Reid kidnapping case like a hot brick the moment he learnt of the Blue Circle painted on Lawrence Reid's door? And of course he was right, for the Reid baby was 'kidnapped' by his wife's maid, who had a weakness for sensation.

In Peter Dewin, the first mention of the Feathered Serpent got a laugh. When he heard of it again, he sneered. Such things, he said, belonged to the theatre, and, rightly speaking, it was in a theatre that the extraordinary story of the 'Feathered Serpent' starts . . .

The applause from the big audience was a deafening blast of sound that roared up to the Moorish roof of the Orpheum and came down again to the packed house like the reverberations of thunder.

Ella Creed came tripping back from the wings, a dainty figure in white and *diamanté*, flashed a smile at her admirers, kissed both hands ecstatically and went off with a little curtsy, only to be recalled again.

She shot one glance at the watchful conductor whose baton went up and fell as the orchestra crashed once more into the opening bars of 'What I like, I like,' that most banal of airs. Ella took centre stage, the chorus came jigging into view for the encore, and for three minutes Ella's shapely limbs were moving with the dazzling rapidity her eccentric dance demanded. She made her exit in a storm of hand-clapping and squawks of joy from the cheaper parts of the house.

She stood for some time, panting, by the stage manager's little desk.

'I want that third girl from the end fired – she's overworking and trying to take it all from me. And what's the idea of putting a blonde in the front row, Sager? If I've told you once, I've told you twenty times, I want brunettes behind me—'

'I'm very sorry, Miss Creed' – the stage manager had a wife and three children and was humble – 'I'll see that the girl gets her notice to-day—'

'Fire her – never mind about notice,' snapped Ella. 'Give her a month's money and clear her out.'

She was very pretty in a small, pinched way; not quite as ethereal as she appeared from the front of the house: the lips were straight under the red cupid bow which a lipstick had drawn.

Ordinary actresses would have waited for the finale, but Ella had a supper engagement and would not line up with the rest of the principals when the curtain rang down – and she was no ordinary actress. She was indeed the proprietor of the theatre in which she acted, the tyrant of a little kingdom which did homage to her nightly and at those *matinées* where she condescended to appear.

She walked through the chorus and they made way for her. A favoured few greeted her with sycophantic smiles, and were rewarded with bare recognition.

Her dressing-room with its silk-panelled walls and shaded lights was a place of luxury. Two women dressers unfastened her flimsy garment; she slipped into a silken kimono and fell back into a chair, submitting to the process of having her make-up removed. Her face was shining with cold cream when there came a knock at the door.

'See who it is,' Ella said impatiently. 'I can't see anybody.'

The woman came back from the little lobby outside the door.

'Mr. Crewe,' she said in a hushed voice.

Ella frowned.

'All right – bring him in. And when my face is finished you can go, both of you.'

Mr. Crewe came in with a little smile. He was a tall, thin man with a hard, wrinkled face; his locks were scanty, and would have been grey if nature had had its way. He was in evening dress, and in the bosom of his white shirt three diamonds glittered.

'Wait till I'm finished,' she begged. 'You can smoke, Billy – give Mr. Crewe a cigarette, one of you. Now hurry up.'

Mr. Crewe, seated on the arm of a big chair, watched the business of changing the make-up of the stage for the make-up of the street without any visible interest or curiosity. Presently Ella rose and disappeared behind the silk curtain which covered a recess. He heard sharp words of reproof and warning: Ella was not in her best temper to-night, he reflected. Not that her moods caused him the slightest perturbation. Very few things disturbed the serenity of this successful stock-jobber; but one of those few things had happened that morning.

Presently Ella emerged. She was wearing a flame-coloured evening gown; about her throat was a rope of pearls, and across her breast a big bar of emeralds that would have been worth a small fortune had the stones been all they seemed.

'Got everything on except the kitchen stove,' said Mr. Crewe pleasantly, when the dressers had made a hurried retreat. 'You're a fool to go out with all that stuff on you—'

'Props,' interrupted the girl nonchalantly. 'You don't suppose I'd run around with twenty thousand pounds' worth of property, do you, Billy? What do you want?'

The last brusquely. He ignored the question.

'Who is the innocent victim?' he asked, and she smiled.

'He's a young fellow from the Midlands; his father has ten mills or something. They are so rich that they don't know what to do

3

with their money. What did you want to see me about, Billy? – this fellow will be here in a minute.'

Mr. Leicester Crewe took from his pocket a note-case. Out of this he drew a card. It was the size of a lady's visiting card and bore no name. Stamped on the centre and in red ink was a curious design – the figure of a feathered serpent. Beneath were the words:

'Lest you forget.'

'What's this – a puzzle?' she asked, frowning. 'What is it – a snake with feathers . . .?'

Mr. Crewe nodded.

'The first one came by post a week ago – this one came this morning. I found it on my dressing-table when I got up.'

She stared at him.

'Well, what is it – an advertisement?' she asked curiously.

Leicester Crewe shook his head.

' "Lest you forget",' he read the line again. 'I've got an idea this is a sort of warning – you didn't send it for a joke!'

'Me!' she scoffed. 'What sort of a fool am I? Think I've got nothing better to do than play monkey tricks? And what do you mean by "warning"?'

Crewe scratched his chin thoughtfully.

'I don't know . . . it kind of gave me a start—'

Ella laughed shrilly.

'Is *that* what you came round for? Well, Billy, you can hop! I've got to meet this boy—'

Ella stopped talking abruptly. She had opened her little gold bag and was searching for a handkerchief, and he saw her face change. When her fingers came from the bag they were holding an oblong strip of cardboard – an exact replica of that which he held in his hand.

'What's the idea?'

She was scowling at him suspiciously.

Crewe snatched the card from her. There was the sign of the

Feathered Serpent, and no word other than the inscription beneath.

'It wasn't in there when I came into the theatre,' she said angrily, and rang the bell.

One of the dressers came.

'Who put this in my bag?' demanded Ella. 'Come on – I want to know who's the joker. Either one or both of you are going to get the sack to-night.'

The dresser protested her innocence, and the second woman, called to explain, could offer no solution.

'I can't fire them because they're useful,' said Ella when they had been dismissed; 'and anyway, it's nothing to lose my head about. I suppose it's an ad. for a film, and we'll see the placards plastered all over London next week. Billy, my boy's waiting.' With a flourishing farewell she was gone.

She had supper at the Café de Rheims, a dancing floor surrounded by expensive menus and London's latest rendezvous. The dull young wool merchant who had escorted her would have seen her home at two o'clock in the morning, but Ella had a perverted sense of propriety and declined his escort. She rented a small and beautiful house in St. John's Wood, 904, Acacia Road, and, like most of its fellows, it was approached by way of a door set in a high garden wall. Beyond, a flagged and glass-covered pathway led to the front door proper.

She said good night to the chauffeur, passed through and closed the outer door. One glance up at her lighted window told her that her maid was waiting for her, and she took two steps towards the door . . .

'If you scream, I'll choke you!'

The words were hissed in her ear, and she stood paralysed with fear and horror. Out of the dark bushes that fringed the path a black figure had emerged, tall, broad-shouldered, menacing.

She could not see the face half covered with a black handkerchief, but, staring past him, she saw a second shape, and her knees gave beneath her.

She opened her mouth to scream, but a big hand closed on her face.

'. . . d'ye hear? I'll throttle you if you make a noise!'

Then everything went dark. Ella Creed, who had simulated faintness so often, had genuinely fainted for the first time in her life.

When she came to her senses, she found herself propped against her own front door. The men had disappeared, and with them her emerald bar and pearls. It would have been a commonplace hold-up but for the card which she found hanging about her neck, attached by a piece of string. And the card bore the symbol of the Feathered Serpent.

II

'Fortunately, Miss Ella Creed was not wearing her jewels, but a very clever imitation of them, so the miscreants gained nothing by the outrage. The police have in hand the card with its crude drawing of a Feathered Serpent, and developments are hourly expected.'

'That's the story,' said the news editor, with the complacency which is particularly characteristic of news editors when they send their subordinates to impossible tasks. 'The feathered snake makes the robbery peculiarly interesting, and brings it into the realms of the sensational novelist.'

'Then why don't you hire a sensational novelist to go out and get the story?' demanded Peter, wrinkling his nose.

He was a tall, untidy young man, with a slight stoop. When his hair was brushed, and he adopted, complainingly, the dress suit, the wearing of which is vital to certain kinds of work, he was singularly good-looking. Nobody had told him so: he would have brained them if they had. They said of him on the *Post-Courier* that he loved crime for crime's sake, and that his idea of heaven was to wear plus-fours seven days a week, and spend eternity investigating picturesque murders.

'This is story-book stuff and doesn't belong to the pages of a respectable newspaper,' he said indignantly. 'Feathered serpent be – blowed! I'll bet you this Creed woman has worked up the stunt for publicity purposes. Ella Creed would jump out of a balloon to get free publicity.'

'Has she ever jumped out of a balloon?' asked the unimaginative news editor, momentarily interested.

'No,' said Peter loudly. 'She may have said she has, but Ella has done nothing more heroic than to eat oysters on the first of September. Honestly, Parsons, can't you give this to the theatrical correspondent? He could spread himself—'

Mr. Parsons pointed awfully to the door, and Peter, who was an experienced journalist and knew just how far a news editor can be baited with safety, slouched back to the reporters' room and moaned his misery to his sympathetic fellows.

On one point he was satisfied: no serpent, feathered or bare, would make him break his engagement. He could only hope that the same ruthless determination was present in the heart of the other party to the contract. Whatever misgivings he had upon this matter were, however, without cause.

When convention and instinct pull different ways, and the subject of the opposing influences is twenty-one and capable, convention is the loser. By most standards, tea-room acquaintances between perfect strangers are attended with certain risks, and 'May I pass you the sugar?' is a wholly inadequate substitute for a formal introduction.

And yet, mused Daphne Olroyd, making a leisurely progress towards the cosy lounge of the Astoria Hotel in the grey of a November afternoon, formal introductions carry with them no guarantee of behaviour. And she was quite sure of Mr. Peter Dewin: much more sure than she was of Leicester Crewe or that red-faced and leering friend of his.

Whether she was cheapened or not by her acceptance of Peter Dewin's attention did not trouble her. She had her own code of values, and the imponderable sense of understanding which told her that the tall young man with the untidy hair thought no less of her because, almost unhesitatingly, she accepted his invitation to tea in a public place.

Peter Dewin was standing square in the middle of the palm court, looking anxiously at the revolving door, when she came in.

'I've got a table as far from the infernal band as I could get – do you like hotel orchestras or do you prefer music?'

He led the way to a corner table, firing over his shoulder

comments on things and people that would have embarrassed her if she had not been amused.

'Everybody comes here on Saturday afternoon . . . no charge for admission . . . that man over there with the horrible waistcoat is a card-sharp – only just got back from New York . . .'

He had a trick of emphasising little points with elaborate gestures; she seemed to be walking behind a human semaphore.

'Here we are – take the low chair – sorry.'

There was nothing furtive about Mr. Peter Dewin. Everybody in the palm court was aware of his presence, even though they might guess wildly at his identity. The waiter knew him, the floor manager knew him, the hall porter knew him. Nobody else mattered.

Daphne learnt of his profession now for the first time, and was interested. Newspaper folk had a mystery for her.

'What do you report?' she asked.

'Crime mostly – murders and things,' he said vaguely, as he fitted a pair of horn-rimmed spectacles to his nose and solemnly surveyed the company. 'When crime is slack – royal weddings, important funerals. I've even sunk to the depths of covering a debate in the House of Commons. Dash these glasses, I can't see anything!'

'Why do you wear them?' she demanded, astonished.

'I don't,' he said calmly as he took them off. 'They belong to a fellow at the office. I collected 'em from an optician.'

He looked round at his companion and surveyed her critically. She did not grow uncomfortable under his scrutiny: she had a sense of humour.

'Well?' She awaited an outspoken verdict.

'You're awfully pretty – I suppose lovely is a better word,' he said unemotionally. 'I knew that when I first met you, of course. I never dreamt that you'd turn up to-day. Was I fresh in the tea-shop? People think I'm fresh when I'm only interested.'

'No, I didn't think you were "fresh,"' she smiled faintly. 'I thought you were – unusual!'

'I am,' he interrupted promptly. 'I never make love to girls; you lose a lot of fun if you make love to girls just because they're girls. You understand that? You miss their humanity and character – you throw away the apple for the sake of the core. That sounds silly, but it isn't. I'm never wholly absurd.'

The waiter came and deposited divers pots and cups.

'You're Crewe's secretary, aren't you?'

She was staggered by the question.

'I saw you once – I came up to interview him about something. I didn't remember that till this morning. One piece of sugar, please.'

He stirred his tea and frowned.

'The older novelists explained why beautiful young ladies occupied humble positions by a bank failure or a gambling father. There have been no bank failures lately.'

'And my poor father didn't gamble,' she smiled. 'I am of the middle class and in my proper sphere.'

He was pleased at this.

'Good. I hate people who've come down in the world. Do you know that woman over there? – she's looking at you.'

Daphne turned her head.

'Mrs. Paula Staines,' she said. 'She's a sort of cousin to Mr. Crewe.'

Peter surveyed the well-dressed lady; she was too far away for him to see her face distinctly.

'Do you like that *ménage*?' he asked abruptly.

'Mr. Crewe's?' She hesitated. 'No – not very much. I am trying to get another position, though I don't imagine that I shall be successful.'

He looked at her sharply.

'Funny, is he? Crewe, I mean. He hasn't the best of reputations. I think that you'd be well out of it. Crewe made his money queerly. It came with a rush, and nobody knows how the money-slide started.'

She laughed.

'Are you very much interested in him, or is this only an extract from—'

'My encyclopædic brain,' he finished the sentence. 'No; I'm interested in him. I'm a crime reporter with a fantastic mind. I have seven theories about Crewe and none of 'em fits. Eat your darned bun!'

Daphne obeyed meekly.

'I've got to go along and give a thousand pounds' worth of free publicity to a lady who has lost ten pounds' worth of jewellery—'

'Not Miss Ella Creed?' asked Daphne in surprise. 'The girl who was attacked in her garden?'

'Do you know her?' he asked.

'No – I've seen her. She sometimes comes to the house. Only Mr. Crewe was rather concerned about the robbery. He had had one of those Feathered Serpent cards the day Miss Creed was robbed. And he was rather worried about it.'

Peter looked at the girl thoughtfully.

'I don't believe there is anything in it,' he said at last. 'The idea has been pinched from—' He named a novelist whom she knew in a dim way as a writer of bizarre stories. 'Thieves are incapable of doing this sort of thing in real life. That "last warning" stuff is bunk, and I refuse to be thrilled. Where are you going?' he asked her abruptly.

She laughed aloud at the question.

'On an even greater adventure,' she answered. 'I'm going after a new job – and I haven't a ghost of a chance of getting it!'

He left her before the busy doorway of the hotel, and took a leisurely route to the Orpheum. At so early an hour he did not imagine that the leading lady would have arrived at the theatre, and he looked forward to a dreary wait; it was a pleasant shock to learn that she was in her dressing-room and would see him.

Miss Ella Creed had evidently just come in, for she was in her street clothes, and her fur wrap still hung about her shoulders. It was the first time Peter had met her, though her companion was well enough known to him.

Joe Farmer was a familiar figure in London. A coarse, stocky man, with a red, bloated face and an ineffable air of prosperity, he was famous principally as a promoter of boxing contests and the proprietor of a chain of public-houses that ran at intervals from Tidal Basin to Kew. He ran one or two horses that were trained in Berkshire; and if his reputation was not of the most savoury kind, he enjoyed a certain frowsy approval which passed for popularity. His big, fat hands glittered like a jeweller's window; he had a weakness for brilliant stones, and a large diamond sparkled in a cravat which would not have escaped attention even had it been unadorned.

He gave Peter a friendly grin and held out one of his big, moist hands.

'This is the very feller you ought to see,' he said. He had a deep, husky voice, and seemed to be suffering from an incurable attack of laryngitis. 'This is the boy! Sit down, Peter, old son. Let me introduce yer, Ella. Mr. Peter Derwent—'

'Dewin, my poor Bacchus,' said Peter wearily. 'D-e-w-i-n.'

Joe Farmer chuckled huskily.

'He's "Peter" to me. Are you coming to see my fight at the Big Hall?'

'Never mind about fights,' snapped Ella viciously. And then to Peter: 'Are you a reporter? I suppose you've come about that disgusting attack that was made on me last night. I must say I was never so frightened in my life.'

She spoke rapidly, and her speech was as unpunctuated as a legal document.

'It's a very good thing for me I hadn't got my real jewellery on. Naturally a lady can't afford to go round wearing ten or twenty thousand pounds' worth of pearls, as you can quite understand, Mr. What's-your-name—'

'Have you the card?' interrupted Peter.

She opened her bag and took out a rather grimy-looking piece of pasteboard, attached to which was a string.

'That's what they found round my neck when I come to,' she said. 'What I'd like you to put in the paper is this: I never lost my presence of mind. If I hadn't been stunned—'

'Did they hit you?' asked Peter.

She hesitated. The desire for publicity was tempered by the knowledge that she had already made a very exact and truthful statement to the police.

'Stunned in a manner of speaking,' she said. 'To be perfectly honest, I fainted.'

'You wouldn't recognise any of the men again?'

She shook her head.

'No, it was quite dark. Usually my chauffeur waits till I've gone inside the house. But like a fool – very indiscreetly – I told him he could go, and that's what happened!'

Peter examined the card with the Feathered Serpent.

'Do you think anybody is playing a joke on you?' he asked.

She brindled at this.

'Joke?' she asked shrilly. 'Do you imagine my friends would play that kind of a joke? No, these men were after the jewels, and I wish I could have seen their faces when they found they'd got "props"!'

She explained unnecessarily that 'props' was a theatrical term indicating imitation jewellery in this case.

Peter heard for the first time the story of the card which had been found in her bag the previous night, and had confirmation – not that he required such – of Daphne Olroyd's story.

'The curious thing is,' said Miss Creed in her breathless, staccato way, 'that my friend, Mr. Leicester Crewe, the well-known stock-broker, also had a card, and—'

'So did I,' Joe Farmer broke in, his face one long grin. 'Say, what do you think of that! Pulling that old stuff on this baby!'

Joe, in his dealings with American boxers, had acquired what he fondly believed to be an East-side vocabulary.

'And listen, Peter – I think I've got a big story for you, one of the biggest—'

'Oh, shut up!' said Miss Ella, sharply if inelegantly. 'We don't want to go into that, Joe.'

So violent was she that evidently she thought it was necessary to offer an explanation.

'Mr. Farmer thinks it's a certain person who's always had a grudge against him and me, but the person is dead, so it can't possibly be *him*.'

The glance she gave to the red-faced man was full of meaning. 'The least said, soonest mended.'

'He may be dead and he may be alive,' said Joe carefully. 'But I've got my own ideas and I'm going to work on 'em – get that! Nobody can put one over on me without a come-back. I'm that kind of guy – I can be led, but I can't be pushed, see? If people treat me right I'll treat them right—'

'Will you shut up?' This time Miss Ella Creed was really angry, and the promoter of fights relapsed obediently into silence.

There was not much new that Peter could learn, and he went back to his office a little puzzled, and to no small degree annoyed. He met the news editor in the vestibule of the office, on his way home.

'There is something in this card stuff,' insisted Parsons. 'And, Peter, I've been thinking since you left. The Feathered Serpent has a peculiar meaning. I went into the library and looked him up in the encyclopædia. He's one of the gods of the old Aztec people. Why don't you go along and see Beale?'

'Who is Beale?' asked Peter, and the news editor groaned. For this was Peter Dewin's weakness, that he was totally unacquainted with any save picturesque criminals, past and present.

'Mr. Gregory Beale is an archæologist,' said the news editor patiently. 'He is also a millionaire. He has just returned from searching for the buried cities of the Mayas; in fact, he got in this evening. I sent a man down to Waterloo to get a story from him, but the darned fool missed him. You'll find his name in the phone directory, and he may give you a good line to the Feathered Serpent.'

He passed out of the building with a cheery good night, and Peter was half-way up the first flight of stairs when the news editor returned and called him back.

'While you're talking to him you might ask him whether

slumland has improved since he went away. He used to be a whale for social reform.'

'If he only came back to-day—' began Peter.

'That's all to the good,' replied Mr. Parsons. 'Invite yourself to accompany him on a trip through the East End. You might get a good column out of it.'

Peter continued his ascent, thoroughly unhappy.

III

London did not hang out its flags on the return to civilisation of Mr. Gregory Beale, though it had in its past done greater honour to lesser men.

He had been a 'story' to newspapers in the days when his chief hobby was the study of the poor and his joy was to dwell in the slums of dockland, a wild-looking Haroun al-Raschid who distributed immense sums to struggling families. None knew this untidily bearded man with the flaming red tie as Gregory Beale, a millionaire twice over. He had a dozen names, changed his address from week to week. Now he would be lodging in Limehouse, now in Poplar. Victoria Docks had known him and East Ham. Then philanthropy bored him – or perhaps he was disillusioned. He went back to his study of the older American civilisations. One day, that section of London which was interested in his movements learnt that he had gone to the Brazils, leading an expedition into the primeval forests. Even this small segment of society did no more than yawn and say that a man with his money should have married twenty years ago. And they forgot him; for he was a man without past connections and a Fabian Socialist. Red neckties, shaggy whiskers and fiery convictions are very wearying to ladies and gentlemen who find their happiness in the belief that the world revolves once in twenty-four hours as a direct consequence of stable government.

Six years after his lawyer took charge of his affairs, the boat express glided slowly into Waterloo station. The line of porters which fringed the platform broke into inconsiderable sections, finally dissolved and was engulfed in the crowd that first surged forward and then, like a colony of ants disturbed in their labours, came into confused and frantic movement.

There were no friends to meet Mr. Gregory Beale, or enthuse upon his lean fitness and the nut-brown shade of his thin face, or smile a response to the good-humour in his bright blue eyes. None to remark upon the obvious fact that he was greyer than he had been when he left London six years before.

John, the middle-aged footman who came shouldering through the crowd to take his employer's suitcase, was too well trained a servant to offer comment upon this evidence of Mr. Beale's strenuous exertions in the cause of science, even if he had any but a dim idea of what Mr. Beale looked like when he went away.

'You're John Collitt?' said Mr. Beale pleasantly.

'Yes, sir – hope you had a good voyage, sir?'

'Very.'

He stood, a dapper figure of a man, whilst the highly polished door of a highly polished limousine was opened for him.

'No, my baggage is being handled by the agency. Home, please.'

He sank back into the springy depths of the seat and watched with eager, almost boyish, interest the common sights that he would have passed unnoticed six (or was it a hundred?) years before. Just little cameos revealed in the uncertain light of street lamps and softened into nocturnal shades by the gathering fog. A man pushing a barrow of rosy apples, a line of brilliantly lighted street cars stretching down the Westminster Bridge Road, the voices of the newsboys yelling their extras, the big illuminated clock towering above the Houses of Parliament and the green of the Park.

Mr. Beale drew a long breath and something sweet and painful gripped at his heart. Home! London was the grey mother and wife that welcomed him – its very indifference to his presence, the immensity which absorbed him as sand would absorb a drop of water, were precious and friendly insults.

The car ran swiftly through the darkness of the Park and into the Brompton Road, turned left and stopped before a large, handsome house that stood on a corner of a wide street. Instantly an oblong of yellow light showed in the gloom as the house door opened and a stout and bald butler came nimbly down the steps.

'Welcome home, Mr. Beale.'

Bassey's voice sounded husky. Was it emotion or age or a cold, Gregory Beale wondered.

'Thank you, Bassey.'

The butler preceded him up the steps; there was something of ceremony in his officiousness. Standing aside to let his master pass.

'There's a young lady in the library, sir. I didn't quite know what to say to her. She says she's come in answer to an advertisement, but I told her that you had only just arrived in England and you couldn't have advertised—'

Gregory Beale shook his head smilingly.

'It is possible to insert an advertisement even on the Amazon,' he said. 'Yes, I did advertise for a secretary. Ask the young lady to come in.'

Daphne Olroyd followed the butler into the long study, and met the scrutiny of as kindly a pair of blue eyes as she had ever seen in a man.

'Will you sit down, Miss – er—?'

'Olroyd,' she said, giving smile for smile. 'I am afraid I have called at an inconvenient time. I didn't know that you had just returned from America.'

'You are with the majority,' he answered, twinkling. 'In this great town I am not sufficiently important to have my comings and goings chronicled. You had a wire telling you to call? Good! That was from Mr. Nunn, my lawyer – he has dealt with the correspondence. Apparently the salary I offered was sufficiently generous to ensure a very considerable response.'

Was it imagination on her part, or did she detect a hint of disappointment in his manner and voice? Her heart sank at the thought. She had seen the advertisement by the oddest chance: some unknown friend had cut it out and sent it to her, and she had applied without any great hope that she would be successful in obtaining a post which carried a salary of seven hundred and fifty pounds a year. And then the thrilling telegram had come.

'I think I fulfil most of your requirements,' she said, quick to anticipate any objection he might offer. 'My speed is good; my French, I believe, is excellent—'

'Yes, yes!' He raised his hand reassuringly. 'Yes – er – I'm sure. Where are you working now?'

She told him. Evidently the name of Leicester Crewe conveyed nothing. He asked her why she wanted to change employers, and she hesitated.

'The salary is a big inducement, of course – but I want a change.'

He nodded, and was silent for a long time.

'Very good,' he said at last, and then to her joy: 'You can have the position: when can you start?'

She went out of the house with a step as light as her heart. As she turned to walk quickly through the gloomy street to the main road, a man who had been watching her from the moment she left the Astoria Hotel, crossed the road noiselessly and followed on her trail. His rubber-soled shoes made no sound; she was unaware that she was being followed until, turning a corner, she looked back and saw the dim shape looming through the fog.

Her first instinct was to run, her second to turn and wait for him to pass. But he had stopped too! One moment he was in sight, the next he had vanished in the fog, and she saw the reason.

A little ahead and walking towards her was a caped and helmeted policeman – and the servants of the Feathered Serpent avoided contact with the police.

IV

There were unkind people who said that Mr. Leicester Crewe had found his name in a timetable. There were some who had a dim recollection of him in those down-at-heel days when he was one of the dingy crowd of hangers-on to the kerb-market, an object of suspicion in City police circles. In those days he was just plain 'Billy,' rather a flashily dressed man with no considerable capital, but with an uncanny knowledge of mining stocks.

Mr. Crewe was musing on those kerb days, the narrow streets behind buildings, the everlasting drizzle of rain, the yellow nimbus of street lamps showing through the fog, and hurrying bareheaded clerks.

He winced at the thought of it, and gazed gloomily round the handsome library of the house to which fate and circumstances had brought him. How long would he command this state? Was there some deadly significance in this Serpent fooling?

The hour was six o'clock on the evening which had followed Daphne Olroyd's visit to her new employer. As yet Mr. Crewe was unaware of the impending change in his household staff. He had come home earlier by reason of a rather important engagement. His mind was on this when he unlocked the wall safe and took out a dirty sheet of notepaper covered, uncouthly, with ill-spelt words in pencil. He read and folded the letter, putting it into his waistcoat pocket as his footman came in to replenish the fire.

'The man has not come?'

'No, sir.'

Mr. Crewe pursed his lips thoughtfully.

'You will bring him at once to me,' he said. 'I don't want you to let him out of your sight. He is an ex-convict I once knew – um – before he went to the devil.'

'Very good, sir.'

Ten minutes passed; the silvery chimes of the little clock on the mantelpiece struck the half-hour. Mechanically and unnecessarily Mr. Crewe looked at his watch, and as he did so the door opened and Thomas ushered in the visitor, a bald little man, shabbily dressed, his broken boots bravely polished. A roundfaced old cherub he might have been but for certain wound marks on his unshaven cheek and a certain inherent suspicion in his pale eyes.

'Hugg, sir – Harry Hugg,' huskily he introduced himself.

Mr. Crewe nodded for the footman to go, and, when the door was closed:

'I had a letter from you two months ago,' he said. 'I did not answer it then, because I could not recall the man. Something has recently happened which – er – has made it necessary to get into touch with you. I now remember Lane – was that his name?'

Again Mr. Hugg nodded. He drooped deferentially in the middle of the room. Mr. Crewe did not ask him to sit down: there was no chair for this bedraggled creature.

'Lane – William Lane. Got seven for passin' slush—'

' "Slush"?'

'Forged notes. They caught him in the 'ouse with the plant. He got seven – his first offence too. Old Battersby always gave seven – he didn't know any sentence lighter.'

Thus he libelled an innocent judge, now gathered to his fathers.

'A very quiet feller – Lane. Him an' me was in the same Hall at Dartmoor. They call 'em "wards" – I don't know why. Funny thing, he was never sick or sorry all the time he was servin'. Me and him went into "stir" on the same day. I got mine for bustin' a house down at Wimbledon. An' we both come out together.'

'Did he mention my name?'

Hugg shook his head.

'No, sir, never mentioned nothin'. We got to London, an' I had some relations at Reading, so I asked him to come down with me –

him havin' no home. When we got to Reading I found my friends had moved, so we went on to Newbury – by road. He died at Thatcham – dropped dead on the road.'

He fumbled inside his pocket and produced a strip of paper. Mr. Crewe took it from him gingerly. It was an official document certifying the death of William Lane of no address.

'It's funny – but just before he died, when we was walkin' along the road, he says to me: 'Harry – if anything happens to me, go an' find Leicester Crewe an' tell him not to forget the – what was the expression? Feathered Serpent, that's it!'

Mr. Crewe blinked twice.

'Feathered Serpent?' he breathed. 'You – you are sure?'

Harry Hugg nodded.

'Took me a long time to remember that – me not bein' a scholar.'

'And that was all he said? Nothing about – anybody else?'

'No, sir – "Tell him not to forget the Feathered Serpent." '

The phrase meant nothing to him – it was absolute gibberish. Never before in his life had he heard of serpents, feathered or otherwise. His heart was beating a little more quickly – then there was an association between the dead William Lane and these fantastical warnings. . . .

'When you didn't answer my letter I thought poor old Lane must have been delirious,' Hugg went on, turning his cap in his hands mechanically. 'I was very fond of old Lane – he saved my life in the prison horspital: I'd ha' been dead if it hadn't been for him.'

'And now he's dead.' Mr. Crewe broke his silence jerkily. 'You're sure – you knew him?'

'Knew him!' Scornfully. 'As well as I know my right hand. He was never out of my sight till they buried him.'

'And he's dead – did he leave any relations?'

Hugg shook his head.

'I never heard of 'em. That Feathered Serpent – it's been worryin' me. But he was so serious when he told me – not like a daft man at all.'

Mr. Crewe walked up and down the room, his chin on his breast. These cards with their crude rubber stamp impressions no longer belonged to the category of practical jokes. The attack on Ella had a deep and sinister meaning. Suppose Lane were alive, against whom would he act? Who but Ella and Paula Staines and Joe Farmer – and himself!

He wriggled his shoulders impatiently and turned a look of deepest suspicion on the ex-convict.

'He said nothing else? He didn't stuff you and your gang with a lot of lies about me, eh? Listen, Hugg, I'll pay good money for the truth. Now let's have it. What was the yarn he told you in Dartmoor?'

But Hugg's face was blank as he shook his head.

'Tell us, sir? What could he squeak about a gen'leman like you? Besides, sir, he was an educated man, not like me an' the other old stiffs. He wouldn't talk to the likes of us.'

Crewe had taken his note-case from his pocket and was displaying carelessly the edges of many bank-notes.

'If a hundred is any good to you—'

Mr. Hugg smiled painfully.

'That'd be a life-saver; but I can't make things up – wish I could.'

Leicester skinned two notes and passed them to the man. He felt he was telling the truth – that Lane was dead – but the Feathered Serpents . . .?

'Here's twenty. You needn't come back for any more, because you won't get it.'

The little man seized the money eagerly.

'I've got your address,' Crewe went on. 'If you change it let me know. I will keep the death certificate. I may run across another Leicester Crewe who will be – interested.'

The little man's eyes shone as he took the notes: evidently here was a result of his visit which he did not anticipate. As Mr. Crewe rang the bell for the footman, he took a step forward.

'This Lane was a good feller.' There was a note which was almost defiant in his voice. 'He saved my life at Dartmoor—'

'Yes, yes,' impatiently as Thomas appeared in the doorway. 'Very interesting – goodbye!'

Harry Hugg shuffled out of the room, saying incoherent and disjointed things.

So that was that. Leicester Crewe straightened himself as though a load had been lifted from his shoulders. For a quarter of an hour he stood looking into the fire, his mind revolving about the dead William Lane, and at the end of that time the one ghost that had haunted the past years was laid for good.

He took up an onyx bell-push attached to a flexible silk cord, gazed at the thing reflectively as it lay in the palm of his big hand, then pressed the ivory button. When Daphne Olroyd came into the beautiful room, with its white wood panelling and concealed lights, she found Mr. Crewe with his back to the stone fire-place, a quill toothpick clenched between his teeth, and a look of gloomy brooding upon his face.

He looked round at her absently as though only dimly aware of her presence. There is a degree of prettiness which merges to sheer beauty; and Leicester, who had adopted the jargon of his day, had once called her 'divine' without eliciting either gratification or enthusiasm from the object of his praise. All the attributes of divinity which a faultless skin, big grave eyes and supple body can give to a woman, she had. Her hair was brown, with a fleet glint of gold in it, and Mr. Crewe might rhapsodise upon her hands if he rhapsodised upon anything. But he was a man without any great power of expression, and his mind was too fully occupied with his project to remark certain signs and symptoms of her disapproval which would have been clear enough to another man.

He lifted his head with a jerk.

'You've thought that matter over, Miss Olroyd? The matter which was detaining me is now satisfactorily—' he paused, groping for a word, and came to the obvious 'settled.' 'I have planned to leave London on the fourteenth of this month. We go to Capri for a few weeks, and then I thought of working down to Constantinople—'

'You will have to get another secretary, Mr. Crewe,' she interrupted quietly.

His lips curled up in a smile, though he was not amused.

'That is ridiculous and old-fashioned – good God, you're living in 1925, Miss Olroyd! Why, there are hundreds of men who take their private secretaries abroad!'

'So I've heard,' she answered, dryly enough. 'But it doesn't appeal to me.'

He made an impatient little clucking noise and blinked down at her. There was something very bird-like about Leicester Crewe, a tough, gaunt bird that was something between eagle and vulture. She always thought of him in this way.

'Stuff and nonsense!' he said loudly. 'Mrs. Paula Staines is coming with us.'

And she smiled before she realised how offensive she was being.

'Even that does not make any difference, Mr. Crewe,' she said.

He murmured something about her salary being increased, and named a handsome sum, but she shook her head.

'It isn't the life I want,' she said. 'In fact, I wanted to tell you that I have secured another post.'

Leicester Crewe's nose wrinkled angrily, but he checked whatever unpleasant thing rose to his lips, and it was in the mildest of tones that he answered.

'I'm sorry to hear that – who is the fortunate employer?'

When she told him, he was no wiser.

'Thank you, that will do,' and she made a glad escape.

He was pacing up and down the room, his hands in his pockets, when the door opened and a woman came in. She was something over thirty, tall, well made, a little less slim than she had been when he first met her, and carefully beautiful. Whatever art could do for her attractions had been done well. Paris had contributed her plain dress, the pseudo-simplicity of which was its grossest extravagance.

Paula Staines walked to the fire-place and spread out her gloved hands to the blaze.

'I saw your secretary in the hall. She did not appear as delighted with the prospect as I should have expected.'

'She refused to go,' growled Leicester, and Paula Staines laughed softly.

'I never thought she was a fool,' she said. And then, abruptly: 'Why don't you marry her?'

He stared at her.

'Who's being a fool now, eh?' he demanded roughly. 'What's the idea? Do you want to hold that over me . . . bigamy?'

She laughed again.

'You've got quite law-abiding since you moved to Belgrave Square,' she said. 'I suppose it's the atmosphere. Bigamy! I've known the time when a little thing like that would have made no difference to you, Billy.'

And then her tone changed; she came back to the table where he had seated himself.

'Billy, I'm getting frightened.'

He stared at her in astonishment.

'Frightened? What about?'

She did not answer for a moment, but stood biting her lips, her grave eyes fixed on his.

'Did Ella tell you that the house had been searched before she arrived? Everything in her private safe taken out, examined and put back.'

Mr. Crewe's jaw dropped.

'I don't understand. Why? Wasn't it worth taking?'

She shook her head.

'It wasn't that. Those fake pearls and the emerald bar they took were a blind. They were looking for something else – and they found it!'

He walked to the door, opened it and looked out, then, closing it again, came slowly back to her.

'I don't get this mystery,' he said. 'What was Mr. Feathered Serpent looking for?'

'Ella's signet ring,' was the reply, and the answer sent the blood from his face.

'The . . . the signet ring?' he stammered. 'They got it? Why didn't Ella tell the police?'

Her faint smile was charged with scorn.

'Could she?' she asked contemptuously. 'No, Ella is a wise girl. Shall I tell you something, Billy? If the pearls and the emeralds had been real, they would have been returned. The man who burgled Ella's flat was William Lane!'

His loud laugh startled her.

'Then he did it from hell,' he said brutally, 'for William Lane died two months ago, and I have his death certificate in my pocket!'

He took out a dirty slip of paper and passed it to the woman. She read it word for word.

'I had this from an old convict who was with him when he died. It's a fake, this Feathered Serpent business,' Leicester Crewe went on, 'and I don't believe the yarn about the signet ring – Ella's a born liar. She'd do anything for a sensation.'

'Why didn't she tell the reporters that?' Paula challenged, and shook her head. 'No, my boy, Ella's scared sick.' She glanced at the paper again, and heaved a long, worried sigh. 'That settles William,' she said grimly.

As she spoke, a telephone buzzer sounded in a corner of the room, and Crewe lifted up the instrument. At first so rapidly did the caller speak that he could make neither head nor tail of his communication or guess his identity.

'Who is it?' he demanded impatiently.

'Joe – Joe Farmer. I want to see you right away. I've found something! Is Paula with you?'

'Yes,' said Crewe. 'What have you found?'

'The Feathered Serpent,' was the surprising reply. 'I've unravelled the mystery, Billy! You trust Joe, eh? . . . Always got his eyes open.'

'Where are you speaking from?' asked Crewe sharply.

'Tidal Basin . . . the old spot, eh? I came down here to make a few inquiries. Say, Billy, I've got these reporter guys skinned to death! Just hang on and wait for me: I'll be with you in twenty minutes.'

Crewe heard the click of the receiver as it was hung up, and passed the gist of the conversation to the girl.

'Joe!' scoffed Crewe, but she shook her head.

'Don't despise Joe – you haven't forgotten that in the old days he was the "finder" of our little party?'

Leicester Crewe made no reply to this. She saw he was more troubled than he admitted.

'If I thought—' he began.

'If you thought what? If you thought there was real danger, you'd get out.' A faint smile played on her carmine lips. 'Billy, you haven't changed very much, have you? I'd like to bet you're all ready for a getaway.'

Instinctively his eyes went to the little wall safe, and she laughed aloud.

'Money, passport, everything!' she mocked. 'What a quitter you are!'

'It isn't the Feathered Serpent or any rubbish like that,' he protested gruffly. 'Only I've had a feeling lately, ever since I had the letter from this lag, that there was going to be trouble.'

'Ever since William Lane was due for release,' she interpreted his thoughts only too accurately. 'But I've never worried about William. In the first place, he wasn't likely to discover us, and in the second place, that kind of weakling doesn't kick back. And suppose he knew where we were, what could he do?'

Leicester was not prepared to answer that question, but the match that he held to her cigarette trembled a little.

'You're getting soft, Billy, and you're worrying yourself over nothing. If you cleared out to-night, I should stay on, just to see what happens. I'm a curious woman.'

'You're a fool,' he said irritably, and relapsed into a long silence.

They watched the slow-moving hands of the clock . . . Paula's cigarette was burnt to an end and replaced by another. A quarter of an hour, twenty minutes, half an hour passed, and then they heard in the quiet street the whine of a car and the squeak of its brakes. Leicester drew aside the curtains and peered out into the fog. He saw the dim head-lamps of the car before the door.

'That's Joe,' he said. 'I'd better let him in.'

He walked out into the dark hall and unfastened the front door gently. As he turned the latch, the door was pushed open, as though somebody were leaning and pushing against it. The latch slipped from his hand and the door opened with a crash, as a dark figure fell with a thud upon the carpet.

Looking past him, the startled man saw the car move off and disappear; and then he heard Paula's voice behind him.

'What is it?' she asked. Her voice was thin with fear.

'Switch on the lights,' said Leicester Crewe, and the hall was suddenly illuminated.

Joe Farmer sprawled face down on the floor, his feet extending beyond the doorstep. In his hand he clutched a crumpled card.

Kneeling by his side, Leicester Crewe turned the figure on to its back, and met the wide, staring eyes of a dead man.

Whatever secret Joe Farmer had brought in such haste had passed with him when, from the darkness of the street, an unknown hand had shot him down.

V

The man had been shot down like a dog from behind. Leicester looked at him, stared paralysed at the figure. Mechanically he drew from the hand the card it held . . . the Feathered Serpent!

As he fell, the man's watch had shot from his pocket, and something else. Leicester Crewe gazed stupidly at a square, flat purse, that had a familiar appearance. What a fool Joe was! So he still carried that souvenir! Reaching over the prostrate figure, he retrieved the little leather case, and passed it behind him.

'It's very curious . . . heard no shot,' he mumbled. 'Take this, Paula . . . put it in the fire or something, before the police come.'

The purse was taken from his hand. He did not turn his head to see who his companion was; did not even realise, when he heard a soft, horrified voice say:

'Shall I telephone for the police? . . . Is he hurt, Mr. Crewe?'

He blinked up at Daphne Olroyd.

'Oh, you!' he said dully.

And then he saw Paula sitting limply on a hall chair, her face white and haggard under the make-up.

'Yes, please . . . telephone.'

Hurrying feet sounded on the stairs that led to the servants' quarters; the footman came into the hall as Daphne went flying up the stairs to her own room. She was dressed for the street, and was on the point of departure when she had been an unwilling witness of the tragedy.

Calling the police station, she told her incoherent and disjointed story: something had happened which she imperfectly understood. She felt that the police sergeant at the other end of the line must have thought she was mad. And then she remembered the untidy young journalist, and after a moment's hesitation searched the directory for the number of his newspaper. She heard herself switched through to the reporters' room, and almost immediately Peter's voice growled:

'Hallo! What do you want? Who is it?'

She was not much more lucid in describing than she had been to the police.

'. . . a dreadful thing has happened . . . I think the man is dead . . . he had a card in his hand. Do you remember the Feathered Serpent?'

'Where are you speaking from?' interrupted Peter quickly.

'Mr. Crewe's house. The man is called Farmer – I'm almost sure, but I didn't see his face – it is horrible . . .!'

'Is he dead?' asked Peter. 'He had a card, did he? The Feathered Serpent? I'll come up right away.'

And then, in a panic, she remembered.

'Please don't tell Mr. Crewe that I told you about this!'

'Trust me,' said Peter's buoyant voice. She had never realised how joyous it could sound.

Then she heard her name called sharply, and ran down the stairs.

'Paula has fainted – she's in the library – look after her.'

Crewe's voice was husky, his manner wild, he seemed on the point of collapse.

There was a little group about the stricken man. Apparently one of the footmen had some knowledge of first-aid, and he was examining the wound. She heard him say something about 'through the heart,' and shuddered as she ran into the library and closed the door behind her.

The woman was lying on the sofa, a pallid, limp figure. Daphne looked at her helplessly. She had never had to deal with fainting ladies, but she seemed to remember that one ought to put their heads between their knees, and this she did . . . gingerly. Whether it was her treatment, or whether Paula was on the point of recovery when Daphne arrived, she opened her eyes and looked strangely at the girl.

'Joe's killed,' she said, and, covering her face with her hands, fell into a fit of hysterical weeping.

Afterwards, sorting out her nightmare memories, Daphne had an idea that she went in search of Crewe and called him into the room. His face was twitching nervously; his pale eyes wandered from the weeping Paula to the girl. For the moment he was incapable of definite thought or action.

'You'd better get out,' he said at last. 'Go down through the servants' entrance and get away through the mews. The police will be here in a few minutes—'

'Couldn't I be of any service?'

For some reason the question seemed to irritate him.

'Service?' he snarled. 'What use are you? . . . I don't want you around. And listen, Miss Olroyd: if the police ask you questions about whether Farmer was a frequent visitor here, you're to tell them he wasn't – do you understand? I've had business transactions with him naturally, because I am an investor, but he was no friend of mine – I never knew him until last year.'

And then he seemed to remember their previous conversation.

'You're leaving me, aren't you? Well, you'd better leave at once. I'll send you a cheque for your salary . . .'

He almost hustled her out of the room, and she was in the foggy street before she even tried to find an explanation for his extraordinary anxiety.

A small crowd had gathered from heaven knew where at the foot of the steps, and as she came through the narrow thoroughfare which led from the mews, she saw the police tender dash up and half a dozen men tumble out. An ambulance followed almost immediately, and then came a taxi, and Peter Dewin jumped to the pavement before the machine had stopped. She called him by name and he turned.

'Hallo! I was hoping you were out of the place. What happened?'

She told him as much as she knew. She had been upstairs in her little work-room, preparing to go home, when, as she had put the light out, she had seen a car drive up to the door. Her little office was above the hall, a small room next to one which was Mr. Crewe's office proper. Immediately afterwards she had begun her descent of the stairs. The hall was in darkness and she had moved a little cautiously. Mr. Leicester Crewe was mean in little matters, and was something of a crank where electric light was concerned.

She had come to the hall as he opened the door, and she had heard the thud of a man falling. And then Mr. Crewe's voice had asked for a light, and she had seen the sprawling figure lying on the floor.

'Oh!' she said suddenly.

'What is it?' he asked.

'He gave me this purse – told me to put it in the fire or something. I think he thought I was Mrs. Staines. Will you give it to him?'

He took the flat purse from her hand and slipped it into his pocket. His cab was still waiting, as he was reminded by the driver.

'You toddle home,' said Peter. 'Take my cab.'

And then he asked her where she lived. She had a small flat in a residential block near Baker Street, a place of street-singers and mechanical piano-players. Peter slipped some silver into the driver's hand, gave him his instructions and came to the closed door of the taxi.

'Do you mind if I come and see you tonight? Have you the inevitable aunt living with you?'

'Not even the inevitable aunt,' she said. 'I am quite alone, and you can only call at the risk of my reputation.'

He thought at first she was serious, till she laughed.

'Come by all means.' And then: 'I am keeping you from your work.'

He waited till the cab had turned slowly in the road and disappeared before he elbowed his way through the little crowd and ascended the stairs. He recognised the burly figure of Chief Inspector Clarke standing in the hallway, and apparently the recognition was mutual. The detective came out on to the steps.

'I've nothing to give you yet, Dewin,' he said. And then: 'How did you hear about this? We've only just arrived.'

'A little bird told me,' said Peter. 'Is he dead?'

Clarke nodded.

'You'd better see me in the morning,' and he said it in such a tone that Peter knew there was no use in arguing.

He already possessed, however, more information than the inspector imagined. He had that important end of a murder story, the name of the dead man. Moreover, he knew where he had lived. He had occupied a flat in Bloomsbury; Peter had been there several times, and was aware that Farmer lived alone except for an elderly woman who acted as housekeeper and cook and controlled the daily charwomen who were brought in to keep the apartments in order.

Now a newspaper man is as honourable an individual as one could hope to find, always providing he is not investigating a case of wilful murder. Peter's intention, as a chance-found cab crawled through the fog eastward, was to reach the flat before the police, secure by hook or by crook a clue that would throw a light upon the crime; and to do this, he was prepared to sacrifice whatever reputation he had for honesty or straight dealing.

The housekeeper was an old acquaintance, and it was his good fortune to find her on the point of leaving the flat. She was going, she said, to the pictures. Mr. Farmer did not expect to be home until late. She added it was her night off.

'That's all right, Mrs. Curtin,' said Peter easily. 'I'll wait for him.'

The aged Mrs. Curtin admitted him without a qualm. It was not unusual for Farmer's friends to arrive before their host, and Peter was allowed privileges which were denied to other of Farmer's friends.

He waited till the door closed on the old woman, and then he began a rapid search of the apartment. The flat consisted of four rooms and a kitchen opening from a narrow passage, which led to the microscopic hall and the front door. That nearest the kitchen was the dining-room, and yielded nothing but an added respect for the dead Farmer as a connoisseur of good wine. Next to this was the housekeeper's room, which he did not attempt to investigate. The other two rooms were what was evidently Farmer's bedroom, and what a more learned man would call his study, but which Joe Farmer had preferred to describe as his 'den.'

It was the largest room in the flat, and was furnished expensively but in execrable taste. In one corner of the room, and in striking contrast to the gilt and silk brocades of furniture and hangings, was a plain pine desk with a roll top. This he tried and found locked. But plain pine desks with roll tops are built to a pattern, and the first of his keys that he tried turned the lock. He pushed up the sliding top and began a systematic investigation of the desk.

Though semi-illiterate, Farmer was a man of method. He found a thick wad of returns from his various saloons and other enterprises, neatly stacked in pigeon-holes; there were also what were obviously private account books filled with the man's sprawling writing; but what interested the reporter was a drawer which had evidently been built into the desk after its delivery. It was fastened with a patent lock, but by an amazing chance the key was fitted into the lock, and it almost seemed, from evidence which he afterwards discovered, that some time that day Joe Farmer had been examining the contents of the drawer.

He turned the key, pulled open the receptacle, and found it to be steel-lined with a hinged lid of the same metal. There was no lock to this, and, lifting the cover, he was surprised to find that the drawer contained only two folded papers. These he opened and examined.

The first was an architect's plan of what was evidently intended to be a great block of working-class flats. Peter growled his disappointment. He knew that Joe Farmer had his finger in many speculative pies. Evidently this building scheme was one in which he was interested.

The second document consisted of two sheets of foolscap, paged

35

3 and 4. Nos. 1 and 2 were missing. From the manner in which it was set out and the terminology, it was evident that these two sheets formed part of a deposition taken in a criminal case. They ran:

. . . the said William Lane was known to me as a dealer in bad money. In America it is known as 'phoney,' in England as 'slush.' I had made the acquaintance of William Lane in a public-house, the 'Rose and Crown,' of which I was lessee. He told me he had been a sailor and had not often been in England, and he asked me whether I would like to buy some good slush. He said he was a printer and could get me all the fivers I wanted, and that he had passed twenty of these in the West End without detection. I thought he was joking, and I told him I would never dream of committing a crime. He passed the matter off with a laugh, but two days afterwards, when I was in the West End, he came into my private bar and asked the bartender if he would change a five-pound note, and the bartender took the money and gave him change, reporting the circumstances to me on my return that evening. I thought nothing of it till that evening when I was making up my accounts and putting the takings ready to bank. I then remembered the conversation I had had with William Lane, and examined the note more carefully. It seemed perfectly genuine, but I was not satisfied, and as soon as the banks opened I took the five-pound note to the Tidal Basin branch of Barclay's and asked the cashier whether it was genuine. He told me that it was a forgery and that there had been several complaints, and special warnings issued by the police concerning the large number of forged notes in circulation. I took the note at once to Divisional Inspector Bradbury and told him of the conversation I had had with William Lane, and of how he had boasted he could give me notes that would defy detection. The inspector told me to say nothing, and placed a detective on duty in my bar. William Lane did not return, and on the 17th I was informed by the inspector that his house had been raided and that machines for printing forged notes had been discovered.

In cross-examination by the prisoner: It was not true that William Lane had only been to the public-house once to change the five-pound note, and that no conversation had taken place about forgeries. It was not true that the statement he had made in examination-in-chief was a tissue of falsehoods invented by him.

Re-examined by Counsel for the Crown: It would not be accurate to say that he was a friend of Lane's. He had only spoken to him two or three times, and knew him only as a habitué of the 'Rose and Crown.' He did not even know whom he was living with or where he was living, or who were his friends.

Here the manuscript ended. Apparently somewhere was a page missing, and Peter made a very careful examination of the remaining pages, but without success. And then by chance he turned over the second of the sheets and found, pencilled on the back, what was evidently a continuance of the evidence. It was in Joe Farmer's indecipherable handwriting, but it was legible enough to Peter:

I am sure that the man was William Lane because just above his left wrist was the scar of an old knife wound which he said had been inflicted by a negro on one of his ships.

At the bottom of the sheet were three scrawled lines in blue pencil:

A. Bone died 14th February, 1922. Harry the Barman, 18 bis Calle Rosina, B.A., very ill.

Peter Dewin's eyes were bright with excitement. Without hesitation he folded the paper and slipped it into his pocket, took up the plan and opened it again, and was returning it to the drawer when he saw the architect's name and the date, 1917. Why should Joe Farmer keep this plan all these years? Here was a point from which a new line of investigation might start. The plan followed the deposition in his pocket; and at that moment there came a sharp rat-tat at the door. Peter gave a last look round, closed the drawer and pulled down the roll-top desk, before he opened the front door to Inspector Clarke.

The big man's face changed at the sight of the reporter.

'You're a quick worker,' he said. 'Who's here?'

'I'm here,' said Peter calmly. 'The old lady who looked after Farmer has gone to the pictures – there is something pathetic about the attraction of the movies for the lower orders, Clarke.'

'Stop your fooling,' said Clarke, as he entered, followed by a subordinate. 'And turn over anything you've found which is likely to be of value to the police!'

'To tell you the truth,' lied Peter, 'I've only just arrived, and I was contemplating a little burglary when your knock brought me back to the paths of virtue.'

Clarke grunted something uncomplimentary about the morals of reporters, and began a rapid search of the room, Peter moving meekly in his wake.

'I suppose you've opened this desk and gone through every paper?' said the inspector, deftly clicking back the lock and pushing up the cover.

Peter looked pained, as the inspector stooped and picked a blue pencil from the floor.

'Did you drop this?' he asked sardonically.

So the note on the back of the paper had been written recently – why? He had looked for the pencil on the desk, and had not thought to search the carpet. Possibly he had knocked it down in his examination, but it was more likely that Farmer had dropped it. It was a new blue pencil, recently pointed; the little chips of wood dislodged in the sharpening process were visible, and the open penknife on the desk still bore lateral blue marks to testify that it had only been that day brought into use.

'No sign of Feathered Serpents,' said Clarke, when he had completed his search. He was prepared to release a few items of information. 'Farmer was shot dead with an automatic pistol fitted with a silencer. We found a spent cartridge in the middle of the road. He came in a taxicab – the cab was seen at the corner of Grosvenor Square by a police officer as it turned into Grosvenor Street. Crewe thought it was a small car, but his description tallies with the policeman's. The man who killed Farmer was either travelling in that taxi or was the driver. That's for publication,

Peter. What isn't for publication – and I'm telling you this in case you get on to it by accident – is that Crewe had a talk with Farmer on the phone half an hour before he was killed. Farmer said he'd got some information about this Feathered Serpent business, and was coming to tell.'

'Why should they be mutually interested in the Feathered Serpent?' asked Peter.

The inspector looked at him thoughtfully.

'That's a bluff question. You know darned well that both Crewe and Farmer have had these cards. What is the Fleet Street theory about the Serpent?'

Peter shook his head.

'We haven't taken it seriously. It's too much like the invention of a sensational novelist – those things don't really happen; you know that, Clarke.'

'This murder has happened right enough,' said Clarke grimly.

He was still suspicious, and as they walked into Bloomsbury Square he asked:

'You found nothing—'

'I found nothing that could possibly assist the police,' said Peter promptly.

'Which means,' said Clarke after a moment's thought, 'you found nothing you'd give to the police which was likely to help another newspaper to get on to the big story. I'd be doing my duty if I hauled you into Tottenham Court Road police station and "fanned" you.'

By the time Peter had reached his newspaper office he had settled in his mind what line he should adopt in his story of the crime. A few additional details had arrived, and substantially the story he told was the one which appeared in every other journal on the following morning.

Summer and winter, Peter usually spent his weekend at a little cottage on the Godalming road. He would have welcomed the chance of thinking out a fantastic problem in the quiet of the country, but there was no long week-end for Peter Dewin, and he went home to his Kensington lodgings, a baffled and bewildered young man.

Crime, as Peter understood it from long experience, was a very commonplace and unromantic thing. He had yet to report a murder that carried with it the glamour of romance. In nine cases out of ten there was no relief from sordidness, and the business of crime detection was a grim and ugly one, which had none of the bright spots that are found in the inventions of imaginative writers.

He was well acquainted with that variety of fiction where last warnings, mysterious letter-writings, and the appearance at odd places and times of bizarre symbols figured prominently. But hitherto his acquaintance with these exciting phenomena had been restricted to certain police court proceedings against bands of juvenile desperadoes with their secret signs and passwords and petty depredations; somehow he could not associate such happenings with grown criminals.

He was sitting on his bed, taking off his boots, when he remembered with a start the little purse that Daphne had given to him, and he took it from his coat pocket. It was a flat pouch of pliable leather, the flap fastening with a catch button; there was something hard inside. A key, he knew before he put in his finger and took it out, and with it a slip of paper.

The key obviously fitted a patent lock; it was rather small, and had upon the thumb-piece the numbers 7916. It had once borne some sort of inscription, but this had been filed off at some period, obviously by an amateur hand.

He examined the paper; it bore two lines of letters:

F.T.B.T.L.Z.S.Y.

H.V.D.V.N.B.U.A.

It was either a code, or the key to a code. The paper was old; the lettering was in ink, which had already begun to fade.

He searched the purse carefully for a further clue, but there was none, nor did it bear any markings. He was about to replace the purse in his pocket when, for some reason which he never understood, he changed his mind and slipped it under his pillow, and continued his undressing. Dead tired as he was, his head had hardly touched the pillow before he was asleep.

VI

It was a gentle tap against one of the legs of the iron bedstead which woke him instantly. Along the edge of the blind which covered the window was a streak of yellow light that stood for the street lamp outside.

He sat up in bed. The room was in darkness, but outside the door and immediately opposite was a window which looked down into the back court of the house, and there was enough light in the sky to show him that his door was ajar. He strained his ears, listening, and presently he heard a deep breathing. Somebody was in the room.

Stretching out his hand stealthily towards a small electric torch which he kept on the table by the side of his bed, he kept his eyes upon the door and saw it was open. In an instant he was out of bed and had flashed on the lamp.

He caught a glimpse of a figure crouched to spring; saw only the lowered head, thinly covered with greying hair, and then something struck him on the shoulder, so violently that he dropped the lamp, and in another instant was grappling with the intruder. Wrenching himself free, he stooped and picked up the torch that his foot had touched, lashed out wildly, but hit air, and in another fraction of a second he heard the door slam and the key turn.

The whole house was aroused now. Voices called from the lower floors, and he heard the patter of feet on the stairs, as some of the other boarders, alarmed by the sound of the struggle, came on the scene.

It was fully five minutes before the key was found to unlock his door, and by this time Peter had switched on the lights. The room was in some confusion, and the first discovery he made was that the intruder had carried off the jacket which he had hung on one of the bed-posts. His trousers pockets were turned inside out and their contents had vanished, but his watch and chain, which were in his waistcoat, had been left behind.

The burglar had left no clue as to his identity, but his method of escape was obvious. The window in the corridor outside the room was wide open. From here was a short drop to the flat roof of the kitchen below, and thence it was easy enough to reach the courtyard wall and the street.

There was no mystery as to how the stranger came to pick on Peter's room – if that had been his objective. It was a peculiarity of the boarding-house that the cards of the 'guests' were fixed in a little brass holder on each door, and Peter afterwards discovered that, but for this eccentricity of his landlady, he might have been spared a rather unpleasant experience.

Day was breaking dingily when the male guests assembled in the dining-room and drank the coffee which had been hastily prepared by their affrighted landlady. She had sent for the police, to Peter's annoyance.

Nothing was more certain in his mind than that he had been the victim of a haphazard burglary. Some poor, unscientific thief had found access to the house, and had chosen Peter's room because it was the nearest to the window where he had made his entry. This he explained to the local detective-sergeant who called to investigate the crime.

'If he didn't want to take your gold watch,' asked that unimaginative individual, 'why did he pinch your coat?'

'Because he hadn't time to search it,' suggested Peter, but the sergeant shook his head.

'You know these fellows as well as I do, Mr. Dewin. The moment he found he was caught, his first thought would be to get away. He wouldn't load himself up with coats, and he certainly wouldn't have left your watch and chain.'

Later in the morning the coat was discovered by a police patrol in the area of a house off Ladbroke Grove, and it was a curious fact that a silver cigarette-case was still in the pocket, though the jacket had been searched most thoroughly.

Peter heard the news in wonder; but the solution to his little mystery did not come until, turning over his pillow by accident, he saw the little purse, and it flashed upon him that the visitor of the night had been searching for that, and that alone. In his wildest speculations he would not have imagined that Daphne Olroyd was responsible for the burglary, yet that was no more than the truth.

VII

Daphne Olroyd had taken him seriously when he had suggested calling, and she had dozed in her chair till the clock struck one, when she woke with a start and a shiver to the realisation that her little fire had gone out. She was not unreasonably annoyed with Peter Dewin, and her annoyance in this small matter almost overshadowed the memory of the tragic evening. Peter had probably forgotten all about his promise to call – or was it a promise? It was absurd to have expected him at all. What information had he to give of such importance that she could with propriety receive him in her little flat at midnight?

She had her bath and was slipping off her dressing-gown when she heard the bell ring in her kitchenette, and, hastily gathering her gown around her, she went to the front door, never doubting that it was Peter. As she opened the door and switched on the light, she stared in amazement at the caller. It was Mr. Leicester Crewe, though for a second she did not recognise him, so drawn and haggard was his face.

'Can I come in?' he asked abruptly.

She nodded, being for the moment speechless, and closing the door behind him, he followed her to the sitting-room.

'Where's that purse?' he asked.

His voice was harsh, a little querulous. She noticed that the hand which frequently strayed to his face was trembling.

'The purse?'

For a moment she did not know what he meant, and then she recalled the incident.

'You mean the purse you gave me – Mr. Farmer's purse?'

He nodded eagerly.

'Have you got it? It is too bad to give you all this bother. I thought I was handing it to Mrs. Staines, and I didn't remember until afterwards that it must have been you. Where is it?'

She shook her head, and she saw his face fall.

'You haven't got it?' His voice was a croak. 'You gave it to – the police?'

'I gave it to Mr. Dewin—' she began.

'The reporter? Why did you give it to him?' he demanded angrily.

'I asked him if he would hand it to the police,' she said. 'I met him outside the house. Didn't he give it to the police?'

There was a dead silence. Leicester Crewe was absolutely sure in his mind that the purse had not been handed over to Inspector Clarke, because he had seen the contents of the dead man's pockets arrayed on his library table whilst they were being catalogued by a police officer.

'Did you – look inside the purse?' he asked jerkily.

She shook her head.

'No, I only handled it. I thought there might have been a key inside; it felt like that. In any case, I should not have opened it. And even if I had been curious there was no time to examine it. I gave it to Mr. Dewin the moment I saw him.'

His mind was precariously balanced between panic and fury; his hand was trembling more violently, his lean, unpleasant face was twitching.

'The reporter, eh? . . . Who told you to give it to the reporter, eh? It was nothing important, only . . . I think it belongs to me. It was something Farmer wanted me to keep. Do you remember what I told you to do with it?'

It was on the tip of her tongue to say that she had been ordered to put the purse and its contents into the fire, but, obeying a warning instinct, she shook her head. It was not easy to lie; harder now, with his keen, suspicious eyes fixed upon hers.

'Where does he live, this fellow – Dewin?' he asked huskily.

46

'I don't know. I think he's on the telephone – Peter Dewin. He lodges somewhere in Kensington, but he has a phone number of his own.'

Leicester Crewe licked his dry lips.

'You didn't tell him anything about – what I said? About burning – I mean, you don't remember what I said, of course!'

The man was off his balance, confused of speech and mind. She read here evidence of an overmastering fear. His terror almost frightened her. And then, as though he realised the impression he was creating, he gained control of himself and, with an air of disparagement, looked round the room.

'This is where you live, eh? Not much of a show,' he said with an assumption of his old-time arrogance. 'Well, I'll get along. I'm sorry to have disturbed you, Miss Olroyd.'

Until that moment he had not seemed to be conscious of her as an individual, but now she saw the vacant eyes grow a little more human.

'Not a palace you're living in, is it?' he asked in his jerky way. 'Don't you think you're a silly little fool not to stay on with me? I'll be going abroad soon – next week, I think. This affair has got on my nerves, and I'll be away for a long time. Maybe I'll winter in Africa – Durban's a great place. . . .'

She cut the conversation short by walking out of the room and opening the front door to him.

'Possibly I shall be seeing you in the morning,' he said, by no means rebuffed. 'In the telephone book, is he? I suppose you're wondering why I make all this fuss over a tuppenny ha'penny purse? Well, the fact is—'

He stopped; he was a slow inventor, and could think of no plausible explanation for his anxiety. He was mumbling something about 'important keys' and 'sensational reporters' when she closed the door on him.

His cab was waiting before the house, and jumping in he was driven back to Grosvenor Square and let himself in. When he came into the library one of his two visitors, worn out by the excitement of the night, was dozing on the settee; the other stood before the fire, staring gloomily into its depths.

Ella Creed turned as he entered.

'Did you get it?' she asked quickly.

He shook his head.

'Get it?' he snarled. 'Get what?'

'Don't be a fool, Billy,' said the actress. 'What you went after was the purse, wasn't it? Did she have it?'

'She gave it away – to Dewin, the reporter.'

Ella's thin lips grew straight and hard.

'Gave it to Dewin, that flash reporter? Now we're in the soup!'

Paula Staines woke with a start at the sound of voices and sat up.

'What is the trouble?' she asked. 'Did you get the key, Billy?'

Ella Creed laughed bitterly.

'She gave it to Dewin,' she said. 'Dewin! My God! Poor old Joe used to say he was the slimmest crime reporter in London, and as smart as any four detectives rolled into one! And he's got the key—'

'Shut up!' snapped Leicester, looking up from the telephone directory he was exploring.

'How did I know she was there – I thought it was Paula behind me.'

Ella's lips curled in a sneer.

'I'd like to bet that that little doll is working the Feathered Serpent gag! You should have fired her out when I told you months ago.'

Leicester Crewe said nothing. His finger went slowly down a page, and presently it stopped.

'Here we are; Peter Dewin, journalist, 49, Harcourt Gardens, Bayswater – that's just off Ladbroke Grove.'

He scribbled the address on a piece of paper and closed the book.

'What are you going to do?' asked Paula.

She had opened her handbag and was carefully smoothing her face with a diminutive powder puff.

'I'm going to get that key – that's the only thing there is to do, isn't it?' he demanded.

'Couldn't you knock him up and ask him—' began Ella.

'Knock him up!' exploded the man. 'What sort of a story is he going to tell Clarke – that I called in the middle of the night to ask for a purse that fell out of Joe's pocket? What's Clarke going to say to me when I tell him that the purse isn't on view?'

He went out of the room and was gone ten minutes. When he returned, he had changed his clothes for a dark tweed suit, and his throat was swathed in a black muffler.

'I don't know whether I'll be able to get it, but I'm going to try,' he said. 'You people had better wait here till I come back. We shall have to agree to some sort of plan. If the key falls into the hands of the police, the truth is coming out – and I want to have a few thousand miles between myself and London before the beans are spilt.'

The two women heard the front door close, and Ella jabbed at the fire viciously with a poker.

'What's the matter with Billy is that he doesn't know when to stay quiet! He's just a scare-cat! Suppose they did know, what proof have they got, and what kind of charge could they bring against us?'

Paula Staines selected a cigarette from an amber case with infinite care, and lit it before she answered.

'Billy's right. There's something big behind this Feathered Serpent. I wish I could get my brain working. It's funny . . . I've drawn every impossible kind of nightmare beast, but I've never put pen to board over a feathered serpent!'

Ella looked at her with a curious respect in her eyes.

'It must be wonderful to be able to draw,' she said. 'Where did you learn, Paula?'

Paula shot a ring of smoke to the ceiling and watched it dissolve.

'My papa taught me,' she said ironically. 'I sometimes wish he hadn't.' And then, in a changed tone: 'Doesn't it mean something to you, Ella? Do you remember anything that happened to Lane that had to do with the Serpent?'

'Lane!' scoffed the woman. 'That sap! He's dead, anyway.'

And then her face clouded again.

'I wish Dewin wasn't on the job – he's the busiest kind of busy I know! Besides, police reporters do things that the police daren't do – what was that?'

It was the faint sound of a bell, and presently they heard the weary footman pass along the passage, and the sound of an opening door and a muffled colloquy. The sleepy-eyed servitor came in a little later.

'There's a man at the door who wants to see Mr. Leicester Crewe. He says his name is Hugg—'

The two women exchanged glances.

'All right, show him in.'

As the door closed, Paula rose from the couch and walked across to the fire-place where Ella was standing.

'He's the man who wrote to Billy,' she said in a low voice; 'the convict who was with Lane when he died.'

Mr. Hugg came in a little diffidently; his smile was at once friendly and apologetic. If his moist face and glassy eyes indicated abstraction, they also spoke eloquently of intoxication.

'Beg pardon, lady. Mr. Crewe here?' he asked somewhat thickly.

Paula motioned the interested footman from the room, and, after he had gone:

'No; Mr. Crewe has had to go out, about the – the crime which has been committed here to-night. You are the man who was with William Lane when he died, aren't you?'

'Yes, miss,' said Hugg. 'That's what I come to talk to Mr. Crewe about – I've seen him!'

Paula stared at the little man.

'Seen him?' she repeated slowly. 'Who?'

'Bill Lane,' said Hugg.

Ella's sharp cry was triumphant.

'I told you so! The swine isn't dead at all!'

The little man shook his head.

'He's dead all right: I've seen him. He *is* dead,' he said emphatically, 'but I've seen him to-night – the ghost of him driving a taxicab. At least, he wasn't driving, he was pulled up by the kerb in the Edgware Road, and I went up and spoke to him. I said: "Ain't you Bill Lane that was in D Ward with me at Dartmoor?" and he said "Yes." Didn't deny he was dead or nothin'! The most mysterious thing I've ever heard tell of. I says: "I'm surprised at you, William, going in for motoring after what that road-hog done to us down at Newbury—" —road-hog I called him,' he said, with the air of one who was coining a memorable phrase.

He swayed a little as he spoke, and the shrewd Ella recognised the symptoms.

'You're drunk,' she said.

Mr. Hugg shook his head protestingly.

'I've had a couple of glasses on an empty stomach,' he pleaded. 'Not drunk, slightly oiled, miss. And I wasn't drunk when I see Bill.'

'Have you been to the police?' asked Paula quickly.

Mr. Hugg's smile was full of contempt.

'Would I shop a man who maybe hadn't "reported"?' he demanded. 'Though whether ghosts report I don't know.'

Ella knew that he was speaking of the duty of ex-convicts on licence to report to the nearest police station.

'I asked him what his graft was,' the inebriated Hugg went on, with increasing solemnity, 'and he told me he was going to "catch" a man who'd done him a dirty trick – a feller named – now what was the name? He used to talk about him in his sleep, *and* about Mr. Crewe . . . Bill, or Beale – some name like that – a feller who'd done him a dirty trick about a serpent, or a snake or something.'

'The Feathered Serpent?' asked Paula.

He nodded his head with drunken gravity.

'That's the man – Beale. Got plenty of money, too. And then I asked him if he'd seen Harry the Lag. Mind you, miss, I never saw him after the accident . . . I was in hospital. . . .'

He rambled on incoherently until Ella stopped him.

'You'd better come back in the morning and see Mr. Crewe,' she said. And then, as a thought struck her: 'Where do you live?'

He gave the address of a common lodging house, and she jotted it down on Leicester Crewe's blotting pad.

When she had closed the outer door on him, Paula came back, a deep frown on her forehead.

'I don't understand it,' she said, and Ella laughed.

'If you don't understand the effect that booze has on a tramp, you'll understand nothing,' she said acidly. 'He's drunk, and he came back to get a little more money from Billy with a new yarn. Billy showed you the death certificate, didn't he? Well, what are you "not understanding" about?'

In her then mood Paula knew by experience that it was a waste of time to argue with the shrewish girl.

'My hat!' said Ella, as she looked in the glass. 'I'll look like an old woman to-morrow, and I've got a *matinée* to get through. How long is that fool going to keep us waiting?'

This question Paula Staines did not attempt to answer.

'I think we are the fools to be here at all,' she said. And then, in a softer tone: 'Poor old Joe!'

But there was no softness in Ella Creed's composition.

'He asked for it,' she said. 'Why did he want to go nosing around after Feathered Serpents? I'll bet, when the truth is known, you'll find that Joe was the only one they were after. Joe's been in more crook games than any man in London, and he's got hundreds of enemies. It's somebody he squeaked on in the past when he was fencing.'

'You're a queer devil.' Paula was surveying her dispassionately. 'You're the one person in the world who ought to be a wreck to-night.'

'Ought I!' Ella turned on her in a fury. 'I've been trying to get rid of Joe for years. Do you know what chances I've had, Paula? Three years ago I could have married a man with a quarter of a million!'

'You could have divorced Joe,' said Paula.

'Divorced him!' sneered the other. 'Do you think I want to advertise the fact that I was married to a cheap crook? Joe's been in jail twice, and everybody knows it.'

The conversation languished. Paula settled herself again in a corner of the settee, but though her eyes were closed she was not asleep, and was the first to hear the click of a key as it was inserted in the outer door.

'That is Billy,' she said, and went out to meet him.

Mr. Leicester Crewe presented a remarkable spectacle. His clothes were torn and grimy; there was a big rent in the knees of his trousers, his muffler was all awry, and he had the appearance of having been severely manhandled.

'Don't ask questions,' he said roughly, almost before she spoke. 'I'm going up to change. If anybody comes, tell them I'm lying down.'

In support of these instructions, unnecessary as it proved, he came down ten minutes later in pyjamas and dressing-gown.

'Well, did you get it?' asked Ella.

He shot one baleful glance at her and that was all. And, possibly as a reward for her discreet silence, he addressed the rest of his remarks to Paula.

'I'm soft and out of practice. I tried all my strength to get into the place. Ten years ago—'

He made a clucking noise, as though regretting his disreputable past.

'Did you get into his room?' asked Paula.

He nodded and showed his teeth in a smile which was entirely without amusement.

'I had the devil's own luck,' he explained; 'his name was on the door, and it was unlocked. There was nothing in most of his pockets; I hadn't time to search his jacket before he woke up and started a rough house. I managed to get away just in time, and I'd hardly cleared the house when somebody blew a police whistle. Fortunately I didn't meet a flattie all the way back to Grosvenor Square, except one at Marble Arch.'

'Did you get the key?' Paula ventured to ask.

'I got nothing, I tell you,' he growled. 'Has anybody been?'

It was Ella who supplied the information, and Mr. Crewe listened with growing concern.

'Hugg? Did he come back?' And then, when she came to the more sensational part of her narrative: 'Stuff! Lane is dead: I've got the certificate.'

Yet there was doubt in his voice.

'His tale doesn't quite tally with the one he told you,' said Paula quietly. 'I've been thinking it over. Did he say that Lane died suddenly?'

'Dropped dead,' said Crewe.

'And did he tell you anything about his having been in hospital – Hugg, I mean?'

He shook his head.

'No. He led me to believe there was nothing remarkable in the circumstances.'

He searched the death certificate, and for the first time saw the cause. 'Fracture base of skull: result of a running down accident.'

'I wonder why he lied?' Crewe bit his lip thoughtfully. 'These chaps lie so easily—'

'And so unnecessarily,' said Paula. 'Did he tell you that Lane talked in his sleep?'

It was here that the impatient Ella broke in.

'What's the use of talking about Lane?' she demanded angrily. 'If he didn't talk more sense in his sleep than he did when he was awake, he wasn't much of an entertainment! What's going to happen about that key, Billy?'

He had no plans, apparently: the discussion he had promised was to be postponed.

'You might get it, Ella,' he said suddenly. 'You know the man, and you might be able to kid him along.'

'Suppose he takes it to the police?' asked Paula. 'And—'

'Not he!' interrupted the actress irritably. 'This fellow likes to work things out himself – Joe told me a lot about him. He was the man that got the Sampsons their lifer, and the police knew nothing about Sampson's graft till they read it in the *Post-Courier*. He'll work on that key himself.'

Paula stretched herself wearily.

'I'm going home,' she said abruptly. 'I'll drop you, Ella; my car is in the mews.'

Ella nodded, and the three walked into the hall. It was daylight now, and as Mr. Crewe swung open the door, the cold, raw air of morning came shivering in.

'I wish——' he began, and stopped dead.

Three of the four panels of the door were decorated with cards, neatly held in place with brass-headed drawing-pins. Each bore the design of the Feathered Serpent, beneath which was written a name. On the first was the word 'Billy'; on the second 'Florry'; and on the third 'Laurie.' Nor was this all. Fastened to the card marked Billy was a tiny bow of black crêpe.

VIII

Peter Dewin was told by the maid-of-all-work that a lady was waiting to see him in the parlour, and as soon as he had finished dressing he ran downstairs. The office very often sent early-morning letters by girl messengers, and it was not unusual to discover that the waiting 'lady' was a snub-nosed little girl with an urgent message from the news editor.

When he walked into the drawing-room he had a pleasant shock.

'Good Lord! What are you doing here?'

'I've been here nearly a quarter of an hour,' said Daphne, her lips twitching with amusement at the surprise in his face. 'You might imagine that I've been waiting up all night for you – did you see Mr. Crewe?'

'Mr. Crewe?' he said in surprise. 'Why on earth should I see Mr. Crewe?'

And then, when she told him of her midnight visitor, he gasped.

'Crewe?' It was impossible that the burglar could have been . . . 'Did you tell him where I lived?' he asked.

'I might have done, had I known. I only knew that your name was in the telephone book. I thought he might have called for the little purse.'

'You thought he might have called for the little purse?' he repeated blankly. 'Well . . . he didn't. At least, I imagine he didn't. I don't think it was he.'

'Have you given it to the police?'

Peter thought rapidly.

'I am handing it over this morning,' he said mendaciously. 'The truth is, I had rather a busy night and I'm up a little late this morning.'

He looked at his watch; it was a quarter to ten, and he remembered at that moment that he had telephoned on the previous night asking Mr. Gregory Beale for an appointment, and that the scientist had fixed the hour of ten. He mentioned this fact casually, and nearly dropped when she said:

'We'll go together. I've an appointment with Mr. Beale also. In fact, I am his new secretary, though I doubt whether he wants me quite as soon.'

He sat down quickly and stared at her.

'You don't mean . . . is that the new job you were going after?'

She nodded.

'Then, by gosh, you're in clover! A fellow I know who did a lot of work for him years ago told me he pays like a prince and he's one of the nicest men in the world to get along with. You've left Crewe rather hurriedly, haven't you?'

She hesitated.

'Yes. As a matter of fact, he thought I had better go at once. It was a great relief to me. I'd already written to Mr. Beale, telling him I couldn't come for a week, so probably I shall have a week's holiday. Do you know anything about him?'

'He's an authority on Feathered Serpents,' said Peter solemnly.

He saw her mouth open in astonishment.

'At least, my news editor says so, and my news editor knows everything.'

It was a bright, cold morning, an ideal day for a walk across the Park, but time was precious, and Peter indulged in the luxury of a taxicab. On the way he confessed to her that he had no intention of surrendering the key. But it was rather like Peter that he said nothing about the code he had found in the purse. He had a weakness for his little mysteries, but in the expansive mood which her presence induced, he was never nearer to letting his right hand know what his left hand suspected.

They came to Gregory Beale's handsome house as the clock was striking ten, and were admitted by the grave butler, and shown into the little drawing-room. Mr. Beale gave his new secretary precedence, and she found him in the library, where apparently he had consumed a frugal breakfast, for a silver tray was on a side table and a half-empty cup of coffee on his desk. He greeted her with that humorous gleam in his blue eyes.

'Don't tell me you can come at once,' he said, and when she answered in the affirmative: 'Capital! I have been wondering all the morning what I should do with my specimens. They have to be unpacked and classified, and I'm too impatient a man for that kind of work. After what I have read in the newspapers this morning I am most anxious to renew acquaintance with my Feathered Serpents.'

'Feathered Serpents?' she said. 'What are they?'

He chuckled at this.

'You need not be afraid of them,' he said. 'I am not a zoologist! My specimens are mostly implements and statuettes collected from the ruined cities of the Maya, and my feathered serpents are little clay models in which the lay eye would not detect the slightest resemblance either to feathers or serpents!'

He looked past her at the door.

'The young man who came in with you is a reporter, is he not? I think I have killed two birds with one stone.'

He rang a bell, and, when the butler came:

'Ask the gentleman to come in,' he said.

When Peter entered the room the scientist was groping in a bottom drawer of his desk. Presently he found what he wanted, and placed on the table a shapeless little object that looked as if it were fashioned from grey mud. He glanced up at Peter with a nod and a movement of his lips that said 'Good morning.'

'You're the newspaper gentleman who wants to know about the Feathered Serpent? Well, my young friend, here is the veritable article!' he said.

Peter took up the object curiously.

'Be careful how you handle it,' warned the older man. 'That queer little thing is worth anything from five hundred to a thousand pounds. It is a genuine Maya "Feathered Serpent" –

the only one, I believe, that has ever been discovered in a Maya city. A large number have been found in Mexico; in fact, I've brought several back with me, but that is a most venerable Maya, and as such should be treated with respect.'

Peter now saw that the shapeless thing had a definite form; a coiled snake with queer little blobs intended, he supposed, for feathers.

'What is the Feathered Serpent, Mr. Beale?'

The scientist leaned back in his chair, his fingers touching.

'The Feathered Serpent,' he began, and he had something of the manner and style of a lecturer, 'was the ancient Aztec conception of the Creator. He was the First Being. He existed, as they say, "before any two things touched"; in other words, before there was material existence of any kind. He was the symbol of supremacy. He was also a kind of Aztec Nemesis. You may judge his antiquity when I tell you that to the later Aztecs, those whom Cortes fought and conquered, he was merely a myth, was no longer worshipped in the Aztec temples, and had been entirely replaced by a new hierarchy of gods. Except' – he raised a finger to emphasise the point – 'there has always been a small clique, even in those days – even to-day – of serpent-worshippers. You will be surprised to learn that at this very hour in Mexico and Spain, and even in England, there are devotees of the Feathered One – the Splendid Gold Light – the Breather of Life.'

'A religion?' asked Peter. He was dazed but not incredulous.

'Not so much a religion as a secret society, I believe,' said Mr. Beale, with one of his fleeting smiles. 'I really know nothing about the matter, and I am giving you at second hand knowledge that I have acquired at third hand!'

He touched the bell again, and when the butler came:

'Will you kindly make Miss Olroyd acquainted with the house-keeper? She will tell you where to put your things, young lady,' he said.

Peter waited expectantly. The dismissal had been too pointed to be accidental, and so it proved, for when the scientist came back from the door, which he had closed, he asked abruptly:

'Has anything further been discovered about the murder!'

'Nothing,' said Peter. 'You've read the morning newspapers?'

Mr. Beale nodded.

'It was the Feathered Serpent which interested me – naturally. The Feathered Serpent is a very real and potent force to me. I have never met members of this society, and I haven't the slightest idea as to their *modus operandi*. I said nothing before the young lady because it is not a subject that one should discuss before young people – though I don't think you yourself are very old,' he smiled. 'In Mexico the worship of the Feathered Serpent has degenerated to such a degree that it has become the symbol of certain prison cliques – in other words, it is a sort of fetish, the fetish of certain types of criminal. I haven't heard whether that is the case in England, but I know it is so in several of the South American states.'

'Secret societies in prison?' said Peter in astonishment.

'Why not?' smiled the other. 'Secret societies at best are childish amusements; and Heaven knows, prisoners require amusement! In some of the American prisons there are several kinds of societies, innocuous enough, but they exist, with their passwords and grips and all the paraphernalia peculiar to these associations. I didn't imagine for one moment that there was such a thing in England till I read the account of this crime. You, of course, knew all about it last night when you called me up? I must confess that your wish to talk about Feathered Serpents rather startled me.'

Peter picked up the little clay model again and turned it over in his hand. How many thousands of years ago, he wondered, had some dead Indian fashioned this crude shape? What dark-visaged families had bowed their heads in worship before these four ounces of insignificant clay? It had seen the Great Pyramids of the Aztecs with their temples on top; when this clay was modelled the green stones of sacrifice ran red with blood, and the pitiable procession of flower-decked victims climbed daily upward to death. . . .

He shivered as he put the thing down upon the table and dusted his hands as though to rid himself of its contamination.

'Is this – image supposed to have any malignant influence?' he asked, and Gregory Beale laughed.

'Why, Mr. Dewin, you're superstitious!' he rallied the reporter. 'I suppose you believe in the stories of baleful statues that are attributed with possessing evil qualities, so that the curator of no museum can touch them without dying? I assure you there is no potency in that little bit of dried mud.'

'It is worth five hundred pounds?' said Peter, a little shamefaced, as he sought to draw attention from himself.

Beale nodded. Again he seemed to be enjoying the other's discomfort. Then he became serious of a sudden.

'I have imposed no conditions on you when I told you what any archæologist could have told you, but I should like to ask you, as a special favour, when you print these facts and speculations, that my name should not be mentioned. I hate publicity of any kind, and, as I say, the curator of any museum could have told you as much, and probably more.'

Peter was reluctant to suppress the name of his authority, but when such a request is made of a journalist there is nothing for him to do but to agree and abide faithfully by his agreement.

'I'm sorry you've asked me that, but of course I will not mention your name, Mr. Beale.'

Here the scientist chuckled.

'It would do you precious little good if you did,' he said dryly. 'I am not so well known as an archæologist as I am as an eccentric philanthropist!'

Peter pointed to the bookshelf behind the chair where Mr. Beale was sitting.

'I read the title from here.'

'You might have read three titles,' said Mr. Beale, turning round lazily, and stretching out his hand he drew three volumes from the shelf and put them on the table.

Peter picked up the books one by one. The first was called

'Poverty's Cause: an Economic Examination.' The second had to do with the slum problem, and the third, which appeared to be the least interesting of the lot, bore the plain title: 'Poverty: A Study.'

Gregory Beale sighed and shook his head.

'If we enjoyed the nine months of sunshine that the old Aztecs knew, there would be no slums in England,' he said.

Peter remembered certain hovels in sunny Italy and the indescribable slums of Corsica, bathed in everlasting sunshine, but very discreetly offered no opposition to Mr. Beale's theory.

Mr. Beale's mind was, for the moment, very far away and his thoughts were not the most pleasant.

'On the whole, the forests of Central America and the impenetrable jungles which surround the relics of ancient civilisation, are less heartbreaking than the East End of London,' he said; and Peter, who had not come to discuss sociological questions, tactfully led him back to the Feathered Serpent.

'Do you seriously think that there is any secret society behind this murder, and that the cards which have been sent to various people in London have any sinister significance?'

Gregory Beale looked at him thoughtfully.

'Do you know anything about this man Farmer? Has he a prison record? That is the first thing to ascertain. Other people have had the Feathered Serpents, I understand – have they criminal records also? If I were a reporter dealing with this matter, the first investigation I should make would be along those lines.'

Peter was looking at the little model.

'Is it possible to have this photographed?' he asked.

'I can save you the trouble,' smiled the scientist, as he rose and went to a safe in one corner of the room. 'I have several photographs of Feathered Snakes, and you are at liberty to use any one of them, providing of course that my name is not mentioned. It is not modesty,' he went on, as he untied the fastening of the stout portfolio which he took from the safe; 'but some years ago I suffered from the suggestion that my various incursions into strange fields of research were actuated by a desire to bring myself before the public!'

He laughed softly to himself, as though at a very amusing thought.

'Publicity is not my . . . speciality . . . is that the word?'

IX

Peter left the house without seeing the girl again, and a bus carried him to Fleet Street. No further news of any importance had been received about the murder.

'We've had the usual bunch of clue hounds telephoning,' said the news editor, 'and we've heard from the inevitable lady who saw a tall, dark man come out of Grosvenor Square five minutes after the shooting. And oh, yes,' he said, as he remembered: 'the doorkeeper told me that a little tramp called three times between six and eight this morning, and wanted to sell a story – a chap called Lugg or Mugg. He said the murder was committed by a ghost!'

'He was probably drunk,' said Peter, unconsciously near the truth.

'He was certainly drunk, according to the porter,' said the news editor. 'He said that the murder was committed by an old lag—'

'Eh!' said Peter quickly. 'Is the hall porter on duty now?'

The news editor looked pained.

'You've been six years in this office and the routine of it is as Greek to a Jew. No, he went off at ten, but you'll find his report in the book. If you ask me what book—'

But Peter did not ask. He went down in the lift to the entrance hall and called for the night book. It was the practice of the *Post-Courier* for the hall porter to keep a rough record of people who called after the staff had left the office. The night sub-editor went off duty at half-past four in the morning, and between that hour and the arrival of the day staff there was no person in authority to interview callers, though the sub-editor on duty was within telephone reach if anything remarkable occurred.

Peter turned the pages of the night diary. There was only one entry.

> '6 a.m. Man named Lugg called with reference to Grosvenor Square murder. Drunk. Stated murder was committed by an old convict who was driving a cab. He said the man was a ghost. He was very intoxicated (Lugg). He said he wanted £1,000 for the story. His address is Rowton House, King's Cross. Wanted to sleep on a bench in the hall, but I called a policeman and had him removed.'

Peter made a mental note of the address, and went up in the lift to the editorial floor. It was not unusual for all manner of irresponsible people to call at a newspaper office after a sensational murder; generally they were charged with the wildest kind of 'information,' and there was every reason to suppose that the inebriated Mr. Lugg, if Lugg was his name, came into this category.

But there were two points about the brief story set down in the night porter's book which invited attention. The first was that the supposed murderer was an old convict, and this tallied with the theory of Mr. Gregory Beale; and the second, that he was a taxicab driver.

That the shot had been fired from a taxi, was the police view, and although Peter had put this theory into print, the tramp had called at such an hour and in such a condition that it was impossible his story could have been inspired by a careful perusal of the newspaper.

Mr. Lugg of Rowton House was therefore a person to be interviewed with the least possible delay, and half an hour later Peter was waiting in the large common room of Rowton House, a place of glazed brick and an enormous fire-place around which was gathered the inevitable crowd of frowsy failures that drift to such homes.

There was, one of the officials told him, no 'Lugg,' but a 'Hugg' who had come in late that morning, and was now asleep. Peter waited half an hour before the little man came down, red-eyed and wan, and bearing unmistakable evidence of his overnight carouse. He looked suspiciously at Peter as he came into the hall.

'Oh, a reporter?' he said, and his relief was obvious.

'You thought I was a busy?' laughed Peter, and the little man coughed and rubbed his hand over his bald pate.

'Not exactly,' he said. 'I've got nothin' to be afraid of.' And then: 'What do you want, mister?'

Apparently he had no recollection that he had called at the office of the *Post-Courier*.

'The fact is, I've been on a jag for two or three days, and last night a gentleman gave me a bit of money for some work I did for him, and I went a bit over the mark.'

'You're an ex-convict, aren't you?' asked Peter, and again that suspicion in the man's eyes.

'Yes,' he said shortly, 'but that's no business of yours, is it? What do you want?'

'You saw a man last night who you thought killed Mr. Farmer in Grosvenor Square – you said that the murderer was a taxi-driver.'

Hugg's jaw dropped.

'Who told you?' he asked quickly.

'You did,' smiled Peter. 'At least, you told the doorkeeper at the *Post-Courier*.'

Hugg ran his hand over his head in perplexity.

'Did I?' he said dismally. 'There's no doubt when I get a little drink in me, I talk! Anyway, it couldn't have been the feller I said it was – he's dead – I gave the certificate to a gentleman yesterday. It looked like him. He used to have a little grey moustache . . . but he's dead. He dropped dead in Thatcham, when me and him—' He stopped.

'What was his name?' asked Peter, but Mr. Hugg shook his head.

'I'm not givin' you any information for nothing,' he said emphatically.

'But you have.' Peter Dewin was amused. 'You told me a man dropped dead in Thatcham. Thatcham is a little village near Newbury, isn't it? It must be: there's a race called the Thatcham Handicap run at Newbury races – and I don't suppose a very large number of people have dropped dead in Thatcham in the course of the past ten years.'

Mr. Hugg shifted uncomfortably and avoided the eyes of his interrogator.

'He dropped dead, that's all I can tell yer, and the feller that done it ought to have got ten years.'

Mr. Hugg was a little confused, and seemed unaware of the implied inconsistencies. He was not a novel type to Peter. There is nothing quite so typical in the typical criminal as his passion for unnecessary lying. The furtive cunning of little crooks finds expression in a hundred and one futilities. They will 'cover up' unimportant details with the care worthy of a Machiavelli concealing some great secret of state. This unknown of Thatcham had not died a natural death: of that Peter was certain. He might have met his end in circumstances discreditable to himself, but more likely discreditable to Mr. Hugg. He had not been murdered, but had died as the result of an accident. All this Peter sorted out in an interregnum of silence which lasted only a few seconds.

'What were you doing in Thatcham?' he asked.

'Look 'ere, mister—' began Hugg, but Peter, who knew his man, introduced a sharper note into his voice.

'You can please yourself whether you tell me, or whether I go to the police and find out. You came to my office this morning with a cock and bull story about the murder having been committed by a taxicab driver who was dead, and I want to get the truth of it. You either get talkative, or I'll telephone Central Detective Inspector Clarke.'

For the first time the little man took a human interest in the proceedings.

'Clarke?' he said, in surprise. 'Ain't that perisher dead? He ought to be, the lies he's told about me. He got me my lagging.'

A wreck who was evidently a friend of Hugg's brought him a steaming cup of coffee, which he drank noisily. The effect of the coffee was apparently to brighten his intelligence.

'I'll tell you, guv'nor, and if there's any money to be made out of this, I want it. The chap I thought I saw last night was a feller called Lane, who was in the same ward at Dartmoor; we came out together. I took him down to Reading to my relations, but they'd moved' – he hesitated. 'Well, they hadn't moved, but they didn't want us three – two chaps, I mean.'

'Three,' said Peter. 'Let's have a little truth in the proceedings.'

Again Mr. Hugg was silent.

'There was three,' he admitted. 'I don't know what become of the other feller after the—'

'The accident?' suggested Peter, when the man paused.

Mr. Hugg started guiltily.

'Well, yes,' he admitted reluctantly.

'Now tell me all about the accident,' said Peter. 'You were three ex-convicts "on the road."* To where were you tramping?'

'Newbury.' Hugg was a little agitated. 'You're not police, are you? You are a reporter? Let's have a screw at your card.'

Peter produced a pasteboard, which the man read short-sightedly.

'That's all right. I'll tell you, and if you shop me you'll be a dirty dog! There's a little house just outside of Thatcham, and me and Harry the Lag thought we might "bust" it and get a few warm clothes. It was a bitter cold night, and the house seemed to be empty. William – that's the feller who was killed – didn't want anything to do with it, so we left him out in the road to keep watch, and me an' Harry the Lag broke a window in the

* i.e. tramping.

pantry and got in. There was somebody in the house. We'd got a couple of overcoats when we heard a man shouting from upstairs, and we got away quick – threw the overcoats into the garden and bolted. Mr. Blooming William wasn't where we'd left him: he'd walked on, and we overtook him about a quarter of a mile from the house. It was on one of those narrow country roads with sharp twists, and we were standing there in the middle of it, telling him what a quitter he was and arguing whether we ought to go into Newbury or lay up till the morning, when round the corner and moving at sixty miles an hour, come a motor-car without lights. The only thing I remember was hitting a hedge with my face, and I didn't know anything else till I woke up in the hospital. William was killed, but Harry the Lag got away. The feller who done it on us was the owner of this house we'd busted. He was on his way to Thatcham to find a policeman. I suppose Mr. Crewe put you on to me?'

Peter was silent. There are moments when silence connotes knowledge.

'I had to tell him a lie,' Hugg went on. 'Naturally I couldn't tell him William was killed because we committed a burglary, could I? Be reasonable!'

'How did you know about Mr. Crewe?' hazarded Peter.

'William talked in his sleep, and he was always talking about Leicester Crewe. He had a hell of a grudge against him. I had to fake a story with Crewe about him sending a message – and Feathered Serpents. Always talking about Feathered Serpents in his sleep, that bird was—'

'Feathered Serpents?' asked Peter quickly. 'What did he say about these?'

But Mr. Hugg shook his head.

'Nothing; just mentioned 'em; and a name I can't remember. A queer, foreign-sounding name. And he used to talk about a key.'

He paused, evidently trying to remember.

'Anything else?' asked Peter, tense with excitement.

Hugg nodded slowly.

'Yes, about a big house. I forget what he called it – yes, I remember – the House of the Feathered Serpent! That's what it was called.'

Peter Dewin was too good a journalist to produce a notebook, for the sight of a notebook dries up an interviewee more quickly than the voice of conscience. He had a writing pad in his overcoat pocket, and a piece of pencil, and unknown to the ex-convict, he was taking a rapid if somewhat undecipherable note.

'Do you know anything about William – his antecedents?'

'His what?' asked the puzzled Hugg.

'What did he get his time for?'

'Slush,' was the reply. 'He used to print slush.'

'What was his other name – besides William?'

'Lane – William Lane!'

William Lane! . . . The name was familiar. And then, in a flash, Peter remembered the portion of deposition he had found in Joe Farmer's desk.

And now the pieces in this jigsaw puzzle were fitting together. William Lane was the man who had been sentenced for passing forged bank-notes, and it was on the evidence of Farmer that this dead convict had been sent to the heart-aching dreariness of Dartmoor.

'You told Mr. Crewe this, did you?' And, when the man nodded: 'Did you tell him that there were three or two of you?'

Hugg hesitated.

'I told him there were only two of us. You see, guv'nor,' he admitted frankly, 'I didn't want this bloke Crewe to think there'd be another one of us coming to "tap" him. Harry the Lag knew as much about Lane as I did; in fact, he knew a darned sight more. Lane was ill in hospital, and Harry was a hospital orderly in prison. We were all released the same day, and Harry told me that we'd got to keep by Lane and never let him out of our sight and we'd make a lot of money. Lane tried to slip us once, but Harry was too quick for him. Harry used to say: "We'll make a lot of money out of this bird if we don't lose sight of him." I didn't want to tell Mr. Crewe that, because it would have queered my market. When I come out of hospital they were going to pinch me for the burglary, but the beak let me off because of my injuries. I got a copy of the death certificate, and that was the first time I knew that Lane had been killed.'

'What sort of a man was he – his disposition, I mean?' asked Peter, and the little man shook his head.

'A bit strange. I never quite got the hang of him. When he went in, they tell me he was a nice, quiet man, never spoke to anybody, did a lot of readin' – detective novels mostly. An' then he got sort of wicked gradually. You get that way in prison. A man gave him a punch in the quarries one day, and Lane half killed him – he'd have smashed in his head with a stone only we stopped him. It was lucky that the screw* didn't spot the fight, or William would have lost his marks. Age?' Hugg was vague as to this. He thought the man was as old as himself, or perhaps a little older.

'It's funny I thought I saw him driving a cab – I must have been very soused,' he confessed. 'He's dead all right. The Newbury police have got all his papers and record.'

Peter questioned him further, but added nothing to his store of knowledge. Before he left Rowton House he made arrangements that the man should call at his lodgings that night.

In his hands now were threads which might well lead him to the heart of the mystery. The House of the Feathered Serpent! Was that a figment of dreams, a piece of high imagining? Or was the House of the Serpent that grim convict establishment on the bleak moor?

The more he thought of the Feathered Serpent and the warnings which had been given, the more his practical mind revolted

* Warder.

71

from a cliché which almost every writer of sensational fiction had employed. William Lane had been a rare one for detective novels; he might well have got his idea from a steady perusal of this kind of literature. It certainly did not belong to the conventional criminal.

X

Off Fleet Street is a cheery little club, situate in a converted warehouse, which is the resort of newspaper men, and at this hour of the morning the library was empty. Peter pulled an arm-chair up to the fire, took out the purse and examined its contents.

The key irritated him. There had once been a fairly elaborate inscription on the thumbpiece, and there were still traces of the lettering, which had been obliterated by a file. An amateur had done this: the edges were cut sharp, and the filing had been performed by a clumsy hand, for there were scratches half-way down the shank. Whoever had carried it out, the work was not recent, for the filed places were dull. Probably the awkward workmanship was con-temporaneous with the writing on the slip of yellow paper.

He filled his pipe and began a careful study of the lettering.

$$F.T.B.T.L.Z.S.Y.$$

$$H.V.D.V.N.B.U.A.$$

He had not to study long. Cryptograms were his meat and drink, and the solution of this little mystery was almost instantly found. Reading the letters downwards, he noticed that they were in alphabetical progression, except that the letter between them was missing. He went to a writing-table, took out a sheet of paper from the rack, and filled in the missing letters.

$$F.T.B.T.L.Z.S.Y.$$
$$G.U.C.U.M.A.T.Z.$$

$$H.V.D.V.N.B.U.A$$

73

'Gucumatz.' What significance had 'Gucumatz?'

The club had a small but excellently selected library, and Peter browsed along the filled shelves, and presently found the dictionary he sought, and, carrying it back to the table, turned the pages. Presently he stopped and uttered an exclamation of surprise.

> 'GUCUMATZ. *The name given by the ancient Aztecs, and especially by the people of Quiche (Guatemala) to the Creator (see Popol-Vuh). Gucumatz, known in ancient Mexico as Quetzalcoatl, was invariably represented as a feathered serpent, by which name he is also called. Gucumatz is still worshipped in certain areas of Central America, and possibly the origin of the legend may be traced to the appearance in Mexico at a very early period of a white man with a long beard, the legendary Quetzalcoatl.'*

Peter sat back in his chair and ran his hand impatiently through his already disordered hair. The Feathered Serpent again! And yet apparently Joe Farmer had never heard of its existence, and saw no connection between the word he so jealously guarded – that missing letter code was a favourite one with a certain type of jail-bird – and the Feathered Serpent warnings which had come to Ella Creed.

There was something uncanny about it all. For the first time since he had come into the case, Peter had his misgivings. At any moment now, as he dug deeper into the mystery, his spade might turn up a hornets' nest, with disagreeable consequences to himself.

That morning, as they had driven to Mr. Beale's house, and in a moment of recklessness, he had proposed a little dinner at a well-known Soho restaurant – reckless, because it seemed almost certain that his day and evening would be fully occupied.

He was in some difficulty about Daphne Olroyd. She, who had been an inmate of Leicester Crewe's establishment, and who had seen Farmer from another angle, would be a mine of information: and yet he could not in decency exploit her friendship for his own ends. The thought irritated him a little, until his sense of humour prevailed.

That night, when he met her, he salved his conscience by a frank exposition of his dilemma.

'I ought to use this dinner for extracting every ounce of information you have to give,' he said ruefully. 'It's a horrible thing to have nice feelings when you're covering a murder story!'

She laughed at this.

'I thought I had told you all I knew,' she said.

As to Leicester Crewe, Peter might have been the most expert of cross-examiners without learning much more about the financier than he already knew. He was a buyer of stocks and a fairly successful man. She had no feeling against him except that she resented his attitude towards women.

She had been three years with Leicester Crewe, ever since he had bought the house in Grosvenor Square. Joe Farmer she knew; he was a frequent and very often unpleasant visitor. Joe had a reputation for gallantry to sustain, and the first time she had met him he had tried to hold her hand.

'Who is Mrs. Staines?' asked Peter. 'I'd like to get the whole of that gallery in perspective.'

Daphne shook her head.

'I don't know. She is a great friend of Mr. Crewe's, and a friend of the actress, Ella Creed.'

'All rich people,' mused Peter; 'or, if they're not rich, exceedingly well off. What does Mrs. Staines do for a living?'

'She's a lady,' said Daphne primly, 'and ladies never work! She's nice – I rather like her,' she confessed. 'Mr. Crewe has told me lots of times that she is very clever. I've seen some of her drawings in her flat at Buckingham Gate when I called there with a letter from him, and they impressed me rather.'

'An artist, is she?' asked Peter quickly. 'Does she paint?'

Daphne thought.

'No, I've never seen her paintings. All that I have seen has been black-and-white work. She used to do heraldic and symbolical drawings – those wiggly scrolls that used to break one's heart at school. She has several framed in her sitting-room – she's rather proud of them. There is a marvellous heraldic drawing, half as big as this table, with some beautiful work in it. I happen to know, because I had some mad idea of becoming an artist when I was younger. As far as Miss Creed is concerned I don't know her very well; the only time I have met her she has been rather rude to me. Is she a good actress?'

'She's a successful actress,' said Peter carefully. 'Perhaps that's not fair to her. She's playing in musical comedy just now, and that doesn't give her much chance.'

He considered a moment.

'Yes, I should say she was a good actress. I saw her in a straight play about four years ago, and she was rather wonderful in a sob part – a pathetic and appealing little figure she made. You would never dream that she was capable of giving a dresser hell, and reducing a stage manager to tears! And now,' he said briskly, 'what sort of a day have you had with your new tyrant?'

She was enthusiastic.

'I have been cataloguing the most wonderfully interesting things – spear-heads, little statuettes, pottery, and old arms that Mr. Beale has found in these buried cities of Central America. And four Feathered Serpents!' she said triumphantly.

Peter chuckled.

'You'll be an authority on the subject soon. But how on earth can you catalogue them? You aren't an expert on Aztec civilisation.'

She explained that her work had been done under Mr. Beale's eye, and that her duty was to write little labels and affix them to each specimen in some inconspicuous place.

'A number of them had been labelled already,' she said, and he thought no more of this until, later in the evening, she opened her bag to take out a handkerchief, and a thin paper disc fell on to the table. He picked it up and examined it curiously. It was the size of a sixpence, and had in red the word 'Zimm,' followed by a pencilled number.

'That came off an Aztec lamp which Mr. Beale found at some place with an awful name.'

He was silent for a moment.

'Are you carrying it about as a souvenir?' he asked, and she explained that she had wetted the corner of her handkerchief to remove the label, the gummed surface of which had probably stuck.

But he was not listening to her: his eyes were staring past her at an inoffensive diner – a man with a black beard, who sat in a corner of the dining-room, seemingly engrossed in his newspaper and soup. Curiously enough, though Peter had reason for no-ticing this man later, he was looking through rather than at him now.

Peter Dewin was blessed, or cursed, with a memory that was little short of phenomenal. He was one of those extraordinary beings who could read the column-long speech of a politician and repeat it almost word for word. (Not that he ever read column-long speeches of politicians.) He could set down unerringly the order in which every witness gave his evidence in a case ten years old; the gist of their evidence, the comments of the judge, and the speech for the defence. Always providing he had read the account and had not been an eyewitness.

'What is the matter?' she asked, a little alarmed at his unearthly stare.

'Eh? . . . Oh, I'm sorry.' He came back to reality. 'I was just thinking. What did you say that label came from?'

She told him again that it was an earthenware lamp.

'Remarkable,' he said jerkily. 'They had lamps too . . . queer birds! . . . Lit many a pickled old Aztec up to bed, I'll bet! I wonder if they had clubs? And annual dinners? They used to drink stuff called *tiki* or *miki* or some queer Irish hootch, and if they died nobody ever asked the coroner to investigate.'

'What on earth are you talking about?' she asked, astounded.

'Lamps,' he said, in some confusion. 'It's a queer thing about me, Daphne, that when my mind gets working it can't be turned off. Did I call you Daphne? I'm sorry. I hate fresh young men – I'm young, but I'm not fresh. Let us have some coffee.'

He was bubbling over with suppressed excitement: it required no power of discernment to see this. Something she had said had excited him to an incredible extent. What was it? The earthenware lamp?

'Will you stop being mysterious and tell me what has made you like this?'

He looked at her vacantly, swallowed something, and then began to laugh.

'You're rather a darling,' he said extravagantly, and for one moment she thought he had been drinking. 'And I'm rather a brute to tell you so. But I'm not really being fresh: I'm just liking you very much.'

He went off at a tangent to tell her that she was the first girl he had taken out to dinner for twelve years: she was startled to learn that he was thirty-one.

'And that was only a professional appointment,' he said. 'She was remotely acquainted with the Ricks gang. They forged letters of credit, and got away with over a hundred thousand pounds. I was a boy-reporter at the time.'

He intended no more than to cover his own agitation, but the fact that he immediately interested Daphne was a tribute to the teller and to the narrative. She found herself listening, enthralled, to the story of a great and ingenious swindle. It was some inner-conscious association which brought him to the subject of the Rickses. Something had been said earlier in the evening that had been checked by a brain cell, and had set in motion the mysterious machinery of the subconscious mind.

'. . . It was old Clarke who broke the gang. He was a sergeant then, and it got him his promotion. Ricks shot himself on a cross-Channel boat. Two members of the crowd got away to America; one was brought back, but they never got the real forger . . . Ricks was a perfectly amazing draughtsman, but the police theory was that the work was done by his sixteen-year-old daughter, a very pretty child. They never brought it home to her; she wasn't even charged. She went away to France, to some relations—'

He stopped abruptly, and again he was staring past her.

'Oh, jumping Jehoshaphat!' he said softly.

'What is the matter?'

He was frightening her, and was instantly penitent.

'I'm sorry. Why were we talking about Ricks – who pulled *that* lever, I wonder? Lord! how everything is fitting – even this!'

He took up the little red label and examined it with eager interest.

'May I keep this? It may bring me luck,' he said, and, without waiting for permission, put it into his pocket case.

'But how on earth does that "fit"?' she asked, bewildered.

'One day I'll tell you.' He was rather solemn now. 'I wonder who Whiskers is?'

As they left their table, the bearded man had also risen and followed them to the vestibule. Here he disappeared. Peter called a cab and as they drove away he admitted that his conscience was a little disturbed.

'I've been trying all the evening to make you betray your late boss,' he said ruefully, 'and that's not playing the game. I hate to confess it, but this is the first occasion that I've ever felt my conscience working.'

'But I've not said anything about Mr. Crewe,' she said in astonishment, and, when he did not answer: 'Have I told you anything you did not know?'

'You have told me nothing that I might not have discovered from another quarter,' he replied diplomatically.

He looked back over his shoulder through the little window in the hood of the cab.

'You've done that three times since we left the restaurant,' she challenged. 'What are you expecting to see?'

'It looked like a fog earlier in the evening. I was wondering whether it was thickening,' he answered lamely.

He waited in the entrance hall until he heard her door close, then he went back into the street. The small closed saloon that had followed his cab from the restaurant had stopped fifty yards down the road, and was drawn up by the kerb. It was easy to recognise, because the lights burnt dimly, and they were placed rather wide of the radiator. As he stepped briskly towards the car, it swung in a wide circle and went back the way it had come.

Peter hesitated. The menace, if menace it was, might equally well be directed towards him or to Daphne Olroyd, and this last thought filled him with dismay. There was no question at all, but that the car had followed them from the restaurant, and he was pretty certain that the dark, black-bearded man who had sat in a corner, apparently oblivious of all except the newspaper which half concealed his face, was his unknown trailer.

Should he go back and warn the girl? He dismissed this course instantly. She must not be alarmed. What should he do? He could not sit on her doorstep till morning. And then the absurdity of the situation struck him. The atmosphere of the sensational novelist had caught him, and he was imagining all sorts of diabolical plots launched by sinister and mysterious societies, against – whom? A girl whose only offence was that she was the secretary of a scientist, and had acted in the same capacity to a financier of dubious antecedents?

The little car was out of sight by now, nor, in his drive eastward, did he again so much as glimpse the bearded gentleman who had taken such an interest in his movements.

He stopped at the restaurant and interviewed the proprietor, who was an old acquaintance of his, and, to his surprise, the restaurateur gave him the fullest information about the stranger.

'He's a private detective employed by Stebbings. I don't know his name; he may be Stebbings himself. I've had him here once or twice, and as he's usually watching a customer of mine, he isn't particularly welcome.'

A load rolled off Peter's mind. Private detectives are innocuous creatures, and certainly do not threaten the physical well-being of the people they watch. In England especially, where such sleuths are entirely without power, and are, moreover, suspect by the regular police, their activities are more restricted than in America.

He went on his way to the Orpheum with a lighter heart.

Miss Ella Creed was on the stage when he arrived, and he had to wait in the draughty lobby until one of her dressers came hurrying out to invite him to her room. She looked tired and old, and her first words were a confession that she felt all she appeared.

'What with the *matinée*, and being up half the night over poor Mr. Farmer, I am nearly dead,' she said. 'Give Mr. Dewin a drink.'

She made no further reference to the murder until she had signalled her dressers to leave the room.

'I wish, Mr. Dewin, you'd do me a favour.' She had turned in her chair to face him squarely. 'Poor Joe had a private key of mine, and from what Mr. Crewe tells me, it has found its way into your hands. Can you give it to me back?'

Peter was elaborately surprised.

'Oh, you mean the key in the purse? I was wondering whose it was. Yes, Miss Olroyd gave it to me, and I suppose I should have handed it over to the police. In fact, I would have done this, only it was stolen from me last night by an enterprising burglar—'

'Stolen?' Her voice was sharp, unbelieving.

'Stolen,' lied Peter calmly, 'by a gentleman who pinched my coat. It was in the pocket. I'm wondering if, in his hurry, the purse fell out. And he was in a hurry, as you probably know.'

She accepted this accusation of knowledge for a fraction of a second, and then:

'Why should I know?'

'You may have read it in the newspaper,' said Peter, who knew she could have done nothing of the sort, since no account had been published.

Evidently his explanation was the last one she expected, for it silenced her for a minute.

'It's curious you should have put it in your jacket pocket—' she began at last.

'Very,' said Peter gently. 'I should have stuck it into my boot. I generally carry keys that way.'

She glanced at him with suspicion and doubt, for Ella Creed had no sense of humour.

'It is rather awkward,' she said. 'I mean, about losing the key . . .'

'Does it open your jewel-case?' asked Peter blandly, 'or the shrine of your private Feathered Serpent?'

She was on her feet in an instant.

'What in hell do you mean?' she demanded. 'Feathered Serpent! What's the idea of this Feathered Serpent, Dewin? What's it all about? Do you know what I think?' She pointed a white, accusing finger at him – 'It's a stunt – a newspaper stunt that you fellows are working!'

In some ways Ella Creed was a very transparent young woman, and that she was not acting now, Peter could have sworn.

'Now listen, Miss Creed,' he said earnestly. 'There is no stunt about the Feathered Serpent. Newspapers have many methods of advertising their enterprise – murdering publicans is not one of them. Are you serious when you say that you'd never heard of the Feathered Serpent until you received the card?'

She shook her head.

'Nor Farmer? Had he never heard of Feathered Serpents?'

'Of course he hadn't! You were here the night I got the picture. Feathered Serpents! Stuff and nonsense! Whoever is behind this, they've got to know that they can't frighten me! If they're after money, you can tell them that my jewels are kept at the bank, and if they open my safe a dozen times—'

'They did burgle your house, then?' said Peter quickly. 'They took something besides the imitation emeralds?'

She had said too much and would have passed on, but he was insistent.

'Well—' she hesitated – 'yes! They got into the house, but they took nothing – of value.'

There was that in her tone, in her very hurry to change the

subject, which convinced Peter she was not telling the truth. What was she concealing?

'They took something,' he insisted.

There came a knock at the door, the urgent voice of the callboy summoned her.

'I've got a quick change—' she began.

'What did they take?' said Peter.

'A ring,' she said angrily; 'a trumpery thing not worth five pounds.'

'What kind of a ring – a wedding ring?'

'Wedding be—!' She checked herself. Had he known, he could not have asked a more provocative question. 'A signet ring – an old thing I've had for years. Now clear out!'

He made a discreet retirement to the corridor. Yet there was more to be learnt, though she had said too much and was on her guard. When she came out, dressed for the second part of the entertainment, she waved him away.

'I can't see you again to-night, Dewin. It's no use your waiting.'

He made as though to go, but when she was out of sight he returned to interview her harassed dresser.

'Your young lady is not in her best mood to-night,' he said unscrupulously.

The elder woman sneered.

'Best mood? I'd like to know her when she was!' And her companion gave a sympathetic agreement. 'She's been like a devil to-day,' said the dresser, with a candour not unusual in a dresser when talking of an unpopular principal.

'Did she tell you about the burglary?'

She made a clucking noise.

'All they took was a ring. She used to have it here when she was playing in "Sweeties." I wouldn't have given a pound for it.'

'What was it like?' asked Peter.

The dresser could only give a vague description, but her companion remembered the design.

'It had a sort of shield on it, with three bundles of corn and an eagle in the middle – wheatsheaves, that's what they were. She always kept it in her jewel box. I've seen it hundreds of times. Mr. Crewe told her to throw it in the fire once, but it would have broken her heart to throw away good money!'

Ella's reputation for meanness was public property.

'Have you been with her long?' asked Peter sympathetically.

'Too long!' snorted the first of the dressers. 'And I don't care how soon I leave. I've been dressing ladies for twenty years, but I've never met one like her. I remember her when she was a chorus girl, before she came into money and bought the lease of the Orpheum. She had luck from the very start.'

The dresser bent her head, listening to the faint strains of the orchestra that came through the pass door to the stage.

'You'd better go now, mister,' she said. 'She'll be back in a minute for her first change.'

Peter very wisely accepted the advice, and was out of the theatre before Ella came breathlessly back to her room.

'Get me a sheet of notepaper and an envelope, one of you,' she ordered. 'And ring up Mr. Crewe and ask him for the address of Miss Daphne Olroyd; and hurry!'

XI

Living in a block of service flats, Daphne Olroyd was spared the worry and work of housekeeping. There was a kitchen in the basement, which supplied lighter meals for tenants, and she had ordered and finished a frugal breakfast when the bell rang, and she opened the door to see Peter standing on the mat.

'Is this a return visit?' she asked, as she invited him in.

'It is and it isn't,' said Peter, swinging his hat. 'The fact is, I remembered something I wanted to ask you.'

It was so unimportant a something when he came to it that she knew this was not the real reason for his early morning call.

In truth he had spent a restless night, and at four o'clock that morning it had required all his will power to prevent his dressing and going round to her flat to discover whether his overnight fears had been fulfilled. He could hardly tell her that it was a visit of reassurance, or that he had spent the past eight hours imagining every kind of ghastly consequence which might have overtaken her.

Why he should think this way at all he could not understand. The experience of having the responsibility for another's safety and happiness thrust upon him was a little terrifying. He was not able even to diagnose the condition of mind which made these emotions possible.

'I have had an invitation to supper from – but you will never guess who is my hostess.'

He shook his head.

'Not Ella?' he said at a venture, and was startled when she nodded.

'It is rather staggering, isn't it?'

She went into her bedroom, brought out the letter and handed it to him. It was written on Orpheum notepaper, in the uneducated scrawl which was peculiarly Ella's.

Dear Miss Olroyd, – There are so many things that I should like to talk to you about that I wonder if you would come to the theatre *(this simple word was spelt wrongly)* tonight and pick me up and we could go and have a bit of super together. We have met several times, have we not? I am so worried over the death of poor Mr. Farmer, who was a very dear friend of mine, and I should so like to talk to you. Perhaps you would like to see what it is like back-stage. Will you phone me at my house in St. John's Wood? You will find the number in the book.

Yours sincerely,
Ella Creed.

He folded up the letter and handed it back to the girl.

'She certainly rushed through the spelling class – are you going?' he asked, and she was thoughtful.

'I don't know. Do you think I should? It would be dreadfully uncivil if I refused, but I hardly know her. What do you advise?'

'I don't see why you shouldn't,' said Peter, though he had an uncomfortable feeling inside that there were many reasons why this unexpected invitation should be rejected.

'I'll think about it,' said the girl, as she put the letter in her bag. 'I've nothing to do this evening, and I might as well go. I've never been at the back of the stage before; it should be rather fun.'

This morning there was ample time to walk to Gregory Beale's house, and they strolled across the Park together, two young people who found life rather wonderful; though for the life of him Peter Dewin could see no adequate reason why that day was any more remarkable than another.

'You might have to come to dinner with me to-night,' he said as they were nearing the house.

'You're a very busy man,' she said promptly; 'and I don't want to become a habit.'

'You're the first good habit I've ever acquired,' replied Peter.

She did not laugh, as he expected, and her tone was a little cold when she answered:

'You have not acquired me, Mr. Dewin.' She stopped herself adding 'yet.'

He thought he had annoyed her by some careless remark, but could not recall what it was. She, for her part, was equally surprised at her annoyance, for she was a very sane and normal girl, not given to displays of temperament.

They parted awkwardly, and continuing his journey in gloom, Peter Dewin wondered if he was falling in love, and was panic-stricken at the thought.

He went no farther eastward than New Scotland Yard, and sending in his name to Chief Inspector Clarke, was admitted to a little conference which had begun an hour before his arrival.

'Come in, Peter,' said Clarke, a big, coarse-faced man with a heavy grey moustache, and perhaps the shrewdest member of the organisation. 'We're "Feathered Serpenting"! Perhaps you can give us a new angle.'

'I'll give nothing short of the entire structure,' said Peter promptly, 'and I haven't got that. I came to get information, not to give it.'

'There's precious little information you'll get here,' growled Clarke's second-in-command, the redoubtable Sweeney. 'We've arrived up against a dead end.'

'What did you want to know, Peter?' asked Clarke.

'First of all, do you know anything about a man named Hugg?'

Clarke nodded instantly.

'I got him his last stretch,' he said. 'He's a burglar who was released on licence a few months ago, and is reporting regularly to the King's Cross police station. I know that because I happened to see him in the street the other day, and took the trouble to call for a report. What crime has he been committing?'

'Trying to sell me a story,' said Peter, 'which isn't so much a crime as an act of lunacy. That's Question No. I. Question No. 2 is: Do you know anything about the Ricks gang?'

Sweeney, who was talking to his companion, looked round.

'The forging crowd? I took most of them – all except the girl – I suppose you'd call her a child. Is she in London?'

'She was the real forger, wasn't she?' asked Peter, ignoring the question. 'Was she clever?'

'She was indeed.' It was Clarke who answered. 'She took a gold medal of the Chelsea Society when she was twelve for decorative work, and the old Chief Commissioner at the time, who knew something about art, said she'd have made a fortune as a black-and-white artist.'

'What was her name?' asked Peter.

This had escaped their memory, but Clarke rang through to the Record Office and presently looked up from the telephone.

'Paula,' he said, and Peter's heart leapt.

'Paula, eh? Paula Ricks. Did she do the forging? I seem to remember that she was suspected.'

Clarke nodded slowly.

'There's no doubt about it. She may not have drawn the Bank of England notes, but she certainly drew the French *milles*. The expert who came over from the Bank of France said it was the most beautiful piece of work he had ever seen. It wasn't photography, but sheer drawing and etching, and he said that from the point of view of sheer workmanship the plates the Rickses used were superior to the original. But we could never prove it against the girl, and I'm rather glad. The old man was an expert forger, and had been in the business ever since he was a boy. He'd have got a lifer, sure, if he hadn't shot himself. Do you think she's been drawing the Feathered Serpents?'

Peter shook his head vigorously.

'I'd lay big money against that.'

'Hi!' called Clarke indignantly, as the reporter turned to the door. 'What's the idea of drifting in and asking questions and drifting out again?'

Peter turned back.

'I've got a five-sided aspect to this Feathered Serpent murder,' he said, 'and I think I'm going to get the story. I'll promise you this, Clarke: before it's in print you shall have all the facts in your hand. At present I have got to find a lock that opens with a certain key, and I want to know how Joe Farmer handled that blessed word Gucumatz.'

It was on that line that he made his escape.

XII

He had a number of calls to make, some important, some incidental to and dependent upon the results of earlier inquiries. On the top floor of a large business block in Winchester Street he entered the office of an old-established firm of architects, and asked to see the first of the two names upon the door. The clerk shook his head.

'Mr. Walber has been dead five years. It is now Mr. Denny's business. Would you like to see him?'

Mr. Denny proved to be a thin, short-sighted man, whose manner was more than a little impatient, and who gave the impression that he was very anxious to have the interview over and get back to serious work. Even the magic words *Post-Courier* did not impress him. He was possibly so busy a man that he was unaware that such a newspaper existed.

Peter unfolded the plan he had found in Joe Farmer's desk and which bore the name of Walber & Denny, and spread it on the table before the architect.

'That is one of Mr. Walber's plans,' said Denny promptly as he pointed to certain indecipherable initials in one corner. 'I don't know anything about it. Mr. Walber amused himself by designing monstrosities of this description. What is it? Obviously it is a tenement house. Nine storeys high – good heavens! the London County Council would never agree to that! And elevators.' He pointed to certain blue squares in the centre of the building. 'Who on earth would design elevators for tenements? Nobody but poor Mr. Walber!'

'Do you know whom this plan was designed for?'

Denny did not know, and said as much emphatically. He was

not interested, and although he omitted to state his apathy in certain terms, Peter was under no illusion.

'Heaven knows! Mr. Walber was a good-hearted and foolish philanthropist. He died without a penny in the world. Not that he required money, for he was a bachelor.'

Mr. Denny said this so gloomily that Peter knew that the short-sighted man was certainly no bachelor.

'Mr. Walber frequently made plans of this description for his own pleasure. He had ideas that some day a millionaire would come along and give them practical expression. Millionaires, being a notoriously sane class, never offered him the opportunity to perpetrate such indignities upon the architecture. Is that all?'

Peter folded up the plan, secretly amused.

'You're certain that the plan never came through your office?' asked Peter.

'Absolutely,' said the other promptly. 'It would have the firm's stamp upon it, and we never use that kind of paper.'

He had only the haziest idea as to who Mr. Walber's personal friends were, and generally speaking, was disinclined to continue the interview. Did he know Farmer, persisted Peter, the man who was murdered yesterday morning? Here he succeeded in gaining for the moment a passing interest in the world's affairs. Mr. Denny took down a book, which evidently contained a list of past clients, ran his finger down a list and shook his head.

'There is no Farmer here.'

Peter next directed his steps to the City. In Queen Victoria Street is a quaint Queen Anne building, approached by double flights of stone stairs, which is famous the world over as the College of Heralds. He was here the greater part of an hour, and when he came out there was a new gleam in his eye and a newer jauntiness in his step. One corner of the curtain which hid the mystery of the Feathered Serpent was lifted. He had had an illuminating, if baffling, glimpse of the immense possibilities which lay at the back of this extraordinary crime.

The most delicate task of all now awaited him. No. 107,

Buckingham Gate consisted of two large houses that had been converted into flats. The liveried hall-porter told him that Mrs. Paula Staines was in, or at least he believed so. He accompanied Peter up in the little glass and metal elevator, and obligingly rang the bell of No. 4 flat.

A maidservant answered, and ushered Peter into a small, square hall, hung about with drawings. The impression he had was pleasing; it was the home of one who had an eye for beauty. The hall lights were of Venetian glass; the carpet under his feet was thick and rich; and when the maid came back for him and conducted him to a beautifully appointed drawing-room, he realised that Mrs. Paula Staines was going to be altogether a different proposition from the shrewish little actress at the Orpheum.

She was sitting at a small inlaid table, and before her was a square of white Bristol board, which she had covered with a sheet of paper as he entered. A singularly attractive woman, he thought; lovely in an austere way. She might have been grande dame or great courtesan. He knew her to be still on the right side of thirty, and thought she looked younger.

She leaned back in the padded chair and greeted him with a quizzical smile.

'This is a great honour, Mr. Dewin. Have you come to interview me?'

That touch of the sardonic was entirely in keeping with the character he had imagined. Before he could reply she had taken the concealing paper from the drawing and had passed it across the table to him.

'I am drawing Feathered Serpents – they are rather fun, though they don't look very pretty, do they?'

There were two or three sketches on the sheet of feathered serpents coiled, their heads flung back to strike, feathered serpents in a rope-like mass, studies of heads, one or two sketches to secure the feathered effect.

'Heaven bless you for making things so easy for me!' said Peter fervently. 'For that is the very subject on which I came to see you!'

Her lips curled for a second in a wintry smile.

'I had that idea when I saw your card,' she said. 'But believe me, Mr.—' she looked at the card again – 'Dewin, you have not chosen a very high authority – I had never heard of Feathered Serpents in my life until this dreadful murder.'

She was looking straight at him. They might lie, those grey eyes, but if they were lying now he was much mistaken.

'I suppose your call is about the murder?' She put the board down on the table and shivered. 'It is perfectly horrible!'

He knew just why it was so horrible to this serene woman. If he had been a brute he would have told her then and there. Instead, he asked her about Farmer. Apparently she knew him well enough to be acquainted with his many failings. She made no reference to any of his admirable qualities, and Peter supposed that he had none.

'And now, Mr. Dewin' – she put both her shapely hands on the table, and her eyes narrowed a little – 'what is the real object of this visit?'

Such a challenge could only be met as squarely as it was made.

'I'll be perfectly frank with you,' said Peter. 'I want a new line to the Feathered Serpent.' And when she shook her head: 'You may think you don't know, but I have an idea you do. There was a swindle somewhere long ago—'

'I was not in it,' she said quietly. 'I don't expect you to believe that, but it's true. I won't say I did not benefit by it, but until the last minute, when they found I had to know, I was kept in the dark. I am not going to tell you any more than that.'

'Why do you tell me as much?' he asked.

She considered this question before she answered:

'Because I think you've discovered something – about me. I didn't realise that until you came into the room, and then I saw an expression on your face that told me.'

He nodded.

'Yes – you're Paula Ricks.'

She did not answer, and he repeated the words. Again he saw that fleeting, mocking smile of hers.

'I am Paula Ricks, but is that going to help you at all?'

'You knew William Lane,' he said quietly, and to his surprise she shook her head.

'I have never seen him – I did not know of his existence until he was arrested. Afterwards, of course, I learnt everything there was to be known about him.' She leaned forward a little over the table. 'Is it an offence to be Paula Ricks?' she asked quietly. 'You cannot turn me out of the country – I am British. The police cannot arrest me.'

There was a questioning look in her eyes now as she went on:

'I'll tell you something that the police suspect but nobody knows, and I can be very open with you, because we're alone. I engraved every plate that my father used for the printing of the French forgeries. I thought it was great fun . . . yes, I realised the seriousness of it, but still it was great fun, and I loved doing it. But I've never engraved a plate since.'

He looked round the room, noted the luxury of the appointments.

'You got all this for something, Miss Ricks. I suppose you're not married?' She shook her head. 'You've hardly furnished this place and kept up this style on your earnings as an artist.'

She was a surprising woman, and now she gave him his greatest shock.

'The money I have, this flat, everything, came to me – because I was honest!' she said. 'I should have had exactly the same amount if I had been dishonest; but my possessions are the price of my honesty, and my refusal point-blank to go back to the old life I lived in my father's days.'

He was certain that she was telling the truth. And then, with a little laugh, she went on:

'They tell me you're a great guesser of riddles, Mr. Dewin – guess that!'

She rose abruptly and pressed a bell near the desk.

'I'm going to have some tea, and I'll allow you to join me. Really, I was a fool to be afraid of you, but you rather scared me.'

She stopped as the maid came in and took her order.

'I scared you? How?'

She shook her head.

'I don't know. I was afraid you'd find out who I was. And of course you have, and it isn't so terrible after all. And if I had thought twice about the matter, I should never have been scared. You went to Scotland Yard this morning. Did you tell them?'

He was amazed at this.

'How did you know?'

'For an excellent reason,' she replied calmly. 'I've had you watched for the past thirty-six hours, and I know quite a lot about you! Miss Olroyd is rather a nice girl, Mr. Dewin.'

He saw the laughter in her eyes and was conscious that he was blushing. He was conscious of something else too.

'Not Stebbings – you didn't employ them to watch me?'

'Stebbings himself,' she said, with the greatest coolness. 'Of course you saw him – it is absurd for private detectives to wear beards: it makes them so conspicuous. I told him so.'

The talk was interrupted soon after by the arrival of the maid and a tea trolley.

'It is very dreadful about Farmer,' she said, when the girl had gone and she was pouring the tea for her visitor. 'I didn't like him very much, and I could tell you a whole lot about him, but of course I shan't. You're so clever that you will find all these things out for yourself.'

'Are you being offensive or complimentary?' he asked.

'I don't know – I think a barefaced compliment would be as offensive to you as a direct insult.'

He stirred his cup of tea and lifted his cup, looking straight into her eyes.

'I'll give you a toast,' he said. 'Here's to jolly old Gucumatz!'

The cup fell from her nerveless hand with a crash and her face went suddenly bloodless.

'Gucumatz!' she breathed, staring at him with wide open eyes. 'Gucumatz . . .'

Her bosom was rising and falling quickly. He had touched the raw here. In another second he would surprise her secret.

And then the door opened and the maid came in. A telephone call had come through for her; it was the respite she needed; Paula Staines went out swiftly and was gone five minutes. When she returned, she was her old suave self. Whatever change there was in her appearance was due to her change of dress, for that which she had been wearing had received the contents of the smashed teacup, the pieces of which the maid had removed in her absence.

'Now let us be very sensible,' said Paula. Her voice was almost gay.

'And very truthful, too,' said Peter.

'And very truthful, too,' she repeated, 'on both sides. I confess you rather shocked me, until I realised that you had found the stupid word which Farmer carried about with him. But you startled me terribly – you rather love sensations, don't you?'

'I adore them,' said Peter. 'And talking of Gucumatz—'

'It's a silly word,' she said – 'and I swear I'd never heard the word till a year after—' She hesitated, seeking an explanation.

'After—?' suggested Peter.

'After a Certain Event,' she said. 'What does it mean, anyway?'

Did she know, or was she bluffing? He was inclined to believe that she was ignorant of the significance of the word, and he had support for this view after he had spoken.

'It means the Feathered Serpent,' he said slowly.

She stared at him for a long time, and then suddenly dropped into a chair and covered her face with her hands. When she looked up her face was drawn and haggard.

'Will you come and see me to-morrow?' she said, and held out a listless hand. 'No, no, I don't want to talk any more . . . tomorrow.'

She followed him into the hall and watched him depart, and then she called her maid to her.

'Go to Cook's and reserve two sleepers on the Orient Express,' she said.

The maid, who was apparently used to these sudden moves, responded with a pleased smile.

'And, Nita, nobody must know we're leaving to-morrow morning. You had better pack and get my trunks to the station overnight; and leave word with the hall porter that I shall be away for at least a year. But you need not tell him that until the last thing.'

Paula Staines went back to her table and spent the afternoon tearing up letters and signing cheques to close accounts. There was an axiom which her disreputable father had inculcated, which she had never forgotten. 'Always walk ahead of trouble,' he had said. And trouble was coming thick and fast for those who stayed behind.

XIII

Mr. Gregory Beale's study was a large book-lined room on the ground floor. All that was not bookshelf was dark oak panelling, which stretched to the ceiling; and to the scientist this comfortable apartment was literally a living-room.

He had given Daphne a small room at the head of the first flight of stairs, but the first few days of her engagement were spent almost entirely in the library with her new employer. It was a pleasant room in many ways: a large French window opened on to a small, beautifully kept garden – something of a novelty in this crowded corner of London, where ground is valuable and no man sees an open space but conceives a passion for building garages thereon. It was not a large garden, but was enclosed in the high red walls. The residence was on a corner lot, and one of the walls ran flush with a side street. In earlier times, before he bought the premises, the little doorway in the wall was utilised by tradesmen, but this had been removed and the wall bricked up. At the earnest request of the police, and with some reluctance, he had decorated the top of the wall with a bristling *chevaux de frise* of broken glass to remove temptation from wandering marauders.

Through the window, two steps led to the crazy pavement which bisected the flower beds, still bright with late chrysanthemums; and it was Mr. Beale's pleasure to stroll for half an hour in slippers up and down this pavement, stopping now and then to admire the feathery blooms or to pick dead leaves, which were showing now in increasing quantities.

It was a peculiarity of his that he never had curtains or hangings of any kind in the house, and the folding shutters on each side of the windows were never closed (as he told Daphne the first day she entered there) when he was in residence.

He spoke enthusiastically of the hygienic qualities of sunshine, and was rather a faddist on the subject of fresh air. He could very well dispense with curtains or shutters, for his room was not overlooked, and in this respect he enjoyed complete privacy. He had other little fads: no servant ever entered his room unless he was sent for. Should occasion arise, the butler communicated with him through a small telephone fixed on the wall near to the door of the library. Daphne was solemnly coached in this procedure.

'Not, my dear, that I should mind your coming in,' he smiled. 'You're rather like a ray of sunshine, if you will forgive my clumsy flattery. But I have a horror of being intruded upon. That is why I've had double doors fitted to this room.'

She found him that morning walking in the garden, the stem of a violet between his teeth – he never smoked or drank – his hands clasped behind him, and his first inquiry, to her embarrassment, was of Peter. Just then she was rather annoyed with Peter, quite unreasonably, as she told herself, and she found a pleasure, so paradoxical are women in their urges, in sounding his praises.

'Yes, I'm sure he's clever,' mused Gregory Beale. 'A very nice young man – I know little about the Press, so I'm not competent to pass judgment upon his work, even if I recognised it. He is – um – your fiancé?'

She went hot and red at the question.

'Good heavens, no, Mr. Beale! I've only known him for a little more than a week.'

He glanced at her shrewdly and read in her pink face more than she wished to show.

'You meet people and you like them or you don't like them,' he said. 'I've often thought that unhappy marriages are caused by long courtships. Young people have to be on their best behaviour for such an unconscionable time; they have to pretend to manners and moods which are not exactly normal; and then comes marriage and reaction; they go back to their real selves, and it isn't a pleasant experience for either of them.'

It was curious to hear him moralising on matrimony, and she laughed.

'There is no question of marriage between Mr. Dewin and me,' she said, and, a little mischievously: 'You talk as though you were an authority on the subject, Mr. Beale.'

He shrugged his shoulders.

'Heaven knows, I'm not!' he said, and it was as though a shadow had passed over his face, as he went on: 'I was married once – it was not a happy time for me.'

Even in that short period of their acquaintance she had found him a man of accomplishments. He was something of a metallurgical chemist, and counted amongst his possessions a valuable collection of metal-bearing quartzes. The first day she was there he had crushed a piece of conglomerate in a pestle for her amusement, and with the aid of a small electric crucible had extracted a tiny blob of silver. In going through his papers she had come upon the half finished manuscript of a book, written in his neat, almost microscopic hand, and reading a page to discover what it was all about, found that it dealt with such humdrum matters as wages and the cost of living. He had told her to burn it, to her surprise.

'Last year's dogmatisms are generally silly,' he said. 'When they're ten years old they are revolting!'

On the archæology of South America he was an authority, though apparently he had never written a line upon the subject. He showed her an ancient copy of the Popul-vuh; it was written in Old Spanish and dealt with the superstitions of the Quiche kingdom.

'You would find quite a lot about the Feathered Serpent here,' he said good-humouredly. 'You don't read Spanish? That is a pity. The mind of man has not greatly changed in the past thousand years; he is still a child at heart; he loves childish amusements, childish grandiosity. The elaborate ceremonies which accompanied the Aztec sacrifices aren't more elaborate than the initiation ceremonies of the average secret society. The gods have only changed in name.'

This morning, when she was working, she discovered an addition to the furniture of the library, and one which was by no means an embellishment. It was an old oak door, its rusty hinges still attached, and it was leaning against the wall opposite the window. She saw that one face of it was lined with steel or iron. He told her he had found it in an out-house and had brought it in; it had once been the garden door, now definitely bricked up, and he wanted, he said, to reproduce on its weatherworn surface an old Aztec barbaric painting – another hobby of his.

An interesting companion and as interesting an occupation made the hours fly. When Mr. Beale glanced at his watch and asked her if she intended staying all night, she was surprised that the working day had gone.

If she expected to see or hear from Peter she was to be disappointed. There was no note or message from him when she reached her flat.

Ella Creed had made no mention in her letter as to whether she was to dress. Supper might mean a *tête-à-tête* meal in her house, or a more pretentious affair at one of the night clubs. Daphne compromised by wearing a plain black evening gown and a dark silk Italian shawl, one of the few articles of value that had come to her from her dead mother. An inadequate covering, she decided, when she stepped into a chilly cab, for a north wind blew and a drizzle of sleet was falling.

She was not looking forward with any great enthusiasm to an evening spent with the actress. Their earlier encounters had been brief and a little strained; for Ella was the type of woman who divided humanity into two classes – the dependent and the donatory. Daphne had been distinctly a dependent, and had been treated as such. Now, had she been a royal duchess she could not have expected greater consideration than was shown to her when she arrived at the stage door. An obsequious doorkeeper took her personally to Miss Creed's room, and literally Ella followed her with open arms.

'My dear, how good of you to come! Give Miss Olroyd that comfortable chair, Jessie. Do you mind, my dear, if I change? . . . Is this your first visit "behind"? I'll take you on the stage in a minute.'

Daphne experienced a second's spasm of apprehension, but she learnt that 'on the stage' does not mean in the glare of the footlights. She also discovered that 'behind the scenes' was an obsolete phrase, and that 'back of the stage' was the modern expression.

She had arrived in the interval between two acts – that same interval which had been occupied so tensely by Peter Dewin on the previous night.

All the time she was dressing Ella burbled on.

'We'll go round to the Rapee Club after the show. You're dressed, aren't you, dear? I'm glad of that. I ought to have told you – how stupid of me! . . . You know Peter Dewin, don't you? He was here last night. Such a nice boy! But such a cynic! I do hate cynics, don't you, dear? They see nothing beautiful in life except their own silly ideas. . . .'

Daphne listened and watched. Most of the time Ella was sitting before her glass, dabbing her face here and there and staring fixedly at her own reflection. She wondered why she had been invited, and what was the cause of this effusive greeting. She had a shrewd idea that she had found the solution when Ella came back to the subject of Peter.

'He is a nice boy . . . you know him very well, don't you?' Before Daphne could answer, the actress went on: 'But he's such a leg-puller, if you'll excuse the vulgarity. Do you know, that awful boy has a key of mine and he simply won't give it me – told me a story about a burglar having stolen it. And I happen to know that it wasn't in his coat pocket at all . . . you remember, my dear – a key that poor Mr. Farmer carried around with him, and Billy – Mr. Crewe – gave it to you by mistake?'

She did not press the matter, but Daphne guessed now why she had been invited with such geniality. They knew that she was acquainted with Peter, and imagined, wrongly as she believed, that the acquaintanceship was something deeper than was the case; she was to be employed to persuade Peter Dewin to surrender the key. She was rather amused.

Ella was ready now, and led the way through a labyrinth of passages to a high, open space of gaunt canvas structures which she guessed was scenery viewed from the back. From somewhere near came the sound of fiddles, and Ella hurried her past through a forest of struts to a little desk by the side of the stage, where a restricted view could be obtained of the performance. The stage manager put a chair for her, and there she sat for an hour and a quarter, absorbed in a novel view of the theatre as it was.

She saw stage dancers leave the glare of the footlights, a delighted smile upon their painted lips, and seemingly capable of continuing their performance indefinitely; watched them go back to the call of the roaring audience, and return to the wings to collapse exhausted into the arms of their dressers. She heard a sober and indeed depressing argument between two red-nosed comedians on the advantages of cremation as against burial; and a few seconds later heard the house rock with laughter at their quips and antics.

It was with a sigh of regret that she saw the curtain finally fall, and walked back with Ella's arm affectionately disposed about her shoulder. When they came to the dressing-room, Daphne had a shock. A man was sitting in the chair she had vacated; he was in evening dress and smoking a long cigar, and – the last man in the world Daphne wished to meet that night – was Leicester Crewe.

He had aged in two days; sacs had appeared beneath his eyes; the big mouth drooped pathetically. He had to force the sickly smile with which he greeted his former secretary.

'Hallo, Miss Olroyd! Getting acquainted with the stage, eh? We shall be seeing your name in lights one of these days.'

'You know my friend? Of course you know him – how absurd of me!' began Ella. 'Now, Billy, just entertain Miss Olroyd while I change, and afterwards you can take us out to supper – and pay the bill.'

Evidently this was intended as a pleasantry, for her shrill laughter came from behind the curtained recess where Ella was disrobing.

'Take you to supper, eh?' said Mr. Crewe. 'She's always putting that sort of thing on me.'

Daphne was uncomfortable. She was satisfied that Leicester Crewe's appearance was no accident. It had been arranged that he should be the third party at supper, and the girl resented the subterfuge; resented it more, remembering the man's cool plans for her future. For ten minutes they sat discussing futilities whilst Ella's dressers came and went with towels and pots of cold cream. In the recess was a small dressing-table, which the actress, for a good reason, decided to use. The conversation drifted inevitably to the murder.

'Farmer's death has been a terrible blow to me,' said Leicester, shaking his head. 'I shall never get over it. I've had a procession of police officers in my house; in fact, they live there nowadays; and I've seen reporters by the hundred.'

He looked at her out of the corner of his eyes.

'I must say your friend has not bothered me since the night of the murder, which is rather strange, as he's supposed to be a great crime expert.'

'Which friend is this?' asked Daphne innocently, and the question took him aback.

'I mean Dewin. A good fellow that, but a little impetuous and rather inclined to jump at conclusions. And he's put me to no end of trouble. Do you remember that key business? I didn't tell you at the time, but the key belongs to Ella – to Miss Creed – and she hasn't forgotten to remind me!'

He looked thoughtfully at his cigar.

'I'd give a couple of hundred pounds to have that key back,' he said. 'I don't suppose reporters are very well paid, and a couple of hundred might be a little godsend; or he might use it to buy a pretty present for a friend, eh?'

She was indignant, but she did not rise to the bait.

'It's deuced awkward,' said Leicester. He looked round and lowered his voice; Ella was still in the curtained alcove with her dressers. 'You're a woman of the world, Miss Olroyd.'

Daphne was nothing of the kind, but she did not deny her new description.

'We don't want any scandal. The truth is, that key was the key of Ella's house – do you understand?'

Daphne understood, and was so little a woman of the world that she was momentarily shocked.

'They had been friends for years – now you realise why we want to get it back.'

It seemed a very plausible explanation. Daphne had already half made up her mind to use her influence to recover this incriminating piece of evidence.

'Two hundred pounds or three hundred pounds—' began Leicester, and here she interrupted him.

'I don't think money would count with Mr. Dewin,' she said. 'I'm perfectly sure that if he has the key, he will not use it to hurt Miss Creed.'

'Would you talk to him about it?' urged the man in the same low tone.

She nodded, and at that moment Ella came from the recess. As a compliment to her guest she wore black too, and, save for her startling hands, was jewelless. She turned to the dresser who followed her.

'Run out and see what the weather's like,' she said, and to the girl: 'We haven't far to go. I'm taking her to the Rapee. There's a good cabaret show.'

He nodded his agreement.

'Billy, I hope you haven't been telling Miss Olroyd anything dreadful about me?'

He smiled at this.

'I like you too well to "knock" you, Ella,' he said.

It was all part of the game, and was as though they were speaking well-rehearsed lines. Daphne was not deceived. This revelation of Leicester Crewe's had been agreed upon between them, and she was puzzled to understand it all.

The dresser came back with the news that it was raining and snowing hard.

'Have you got a coat, my dear?' And when Daphne displayed her shawl, Ella shook her head. 'You'll be wet through before you get to the end of the court,' she said. 'Jessie, give Miss Olroyd my red coat. Now don't argue, my dear; you've got to wear it. You'll probably be pulled up by gallery girls who want autographs, because they'll think you're poor little me, but that's one of the penalties of fame, my dear.'

The dresser slipped the coat over Daphne's arms and muffled her to her chin, whilst Ella took the more humble raincoat that was forthcoming.

As they passed down the passage towards the stage door, Leicester said something in an undertone to the woman, and she stopped.

'Why couldn't she come?' she demanded angrily. 'She's in it as much as we all are. Paula's giving herself too many airs lately.' And then, in a louder tone to the girl who stood waiting in the doorway: 'Go on, my dear. You'll find the car at the end of the passage.'

'She telephoned she had a headache,' said Leicester. 'I didn't speak to her, but to her maid.'

Ella bit her lip thoughtfully.

'That's not like Paula,' she said. 'Come along; that damned typist will be getting cold feet!'

They passed down the long, dark court together into the street at the back of the theatre. It was a dingy, slum-like thoroughfare, and deserted save for a loafer who was propping up the wall which gave him some sort of shelter against the penetrating sleet. There was no sign of Daphne or of the car. Ella turned to the lounger.

'Did you see a young lady come out of here?' she asked.

'Yes, miss,' said the man. 'Young lady in a red coat. She got into a car and it drove off straight away.'

Ella uttered an oath.

'I'll fire that chauffeur – call a cab, Billy.'

Two minutes before, Daphne had stepped out of the stage door, run across the wet pavement and through the open door into a car. She stumbled against somebody sitting in the corner, and gasped.

'Oh, I'm sorry. I thought . . .'

At that minute the door was slammed and the car moved on. She leaned forward and tapped at the window.

'Wait, wait!' she said. 'There are more people—'

So far she got when a hand gripped her by the arm and dragged her down into the seat.

'Keep quiet, and don't scream, or you'll be sorry!' said a rough voice.

At that moment the car passed under the light of a street lamp, and she had a glimpse of the man who sat by her side. Only his eyes were visible; the rest of his face was hidden by a coloured silk handkerchief knotted behind his head.

XIV

For a long time Daphne Olroyd sat paralysed with terror, capable neither of movement nor speech. She bit her lip till the pain was an agony to prevent herself from fainting. The car was passing rapidly through the West End streets; snow and rain were falling together, and formed a blur upon the glass so that it was difficult to see plainly the landmarks they were passing; but she knew when they were running along the Thames Embankment; she could see the reflected lights upon the water, for the tide was high. She saw the lights of a tugboat passing slowly down-stream, and heard the deep-throated roar of its siren signalling to a police boat that lay in its track.

They left the river at Blackfriars, and sped through the wilderness of the City. She had a glimpse of the grey bulk which is the Tower of London, and then the car began to thread through a number of side streets, presently emerging into a broad thoroughfare. They passed a big building which she knew was the London Hospital, and it was as they were clearing this that she spoke.

'Why are you doing this?' she asked, and although she tried to keep her voice steady it faltered.

'Don't ask questions. You'll know soon enough.'

After this she relapsed into silence. The buildings began to straggle; they entered a region of fields and factories; one was a soap factory by the unpleasant odour. And then they came to the open country; the way narrowed, and they were running between high trees, and the dim lamps of the car showed a tangle of undergrowth that came down to the very edge of the road. Epping Forest, she decided.

She had no sooner made this decision than the car slowed and turned to the right, following a smooth but narrow road that twisted and turned. She expected this lane to bring them to a main thoroughfare, but it went on and on and on, grew less even of surface, and when it did emerge into the open it was on the outskirts of a small village. Through the window she saw huge steel masts stretching upward. . . . A wireless station of some kind.

A quarter of a mile along the road the car turned again, this time into what was little more than a cart-track. It was so dark now that she could not distinguish objects. Presently the machine stopped, and the man, opening the door, stepped out, giving her his hand to assist her.

She saw what looked to be a concrete cottage, the door of which was immediately opened by a woman, who took her arm and led her along a short passage, terminating in one which ran at right angles.

'Go in there and keep quiet,' said the woman. She had a coarse, hard voice, and when she spoke there was a faint aroma of spirits.

Daphne was thrust into the darkness, a door clanged, and immediately afterwards the room in which she found herself was illuminated by two bulkhead lights fixed in the concrete ceiling, and apparently operated by switches in the corridor.

It was a small room, with concrete walls, ceiling and floor; it was slightly larger than the little bedroom she occupied at her flat, and furnished with an iron bed, which had been made, a table and a chair. On a shelf was a brush, a comb, and a small book. A patch of worn carpet was in the centre of the room beneath the table. Leading out of this chamber was a doorless opening. It was a bathroom, small but completely fitted.

She came back to the 'living-room,' her mind in a whirl, and mechanically picked up the book from the shelf. . . . A new copy of the Bible! There was a newness about everything that surprised her: bed and table were new; even the building itself had not long been erected, and had that cemetery smell peculiar to new structures. She tried the door, which was fitted with a square spy-hole, but it was immovable.

Daphne Olroyd sat down on the bed and tried to order her thoughts. She was trembling in every limb; her teeth were chattering, not with cold, for the room was comfortably warm. She was stunned by the unexpectedness of the outrage; a thousand wild fears criss-crossed her mind, but always, for some unaccountable reason, like a high rock in the tempestuous ocean of her thoughts, she found a mental refuge in Peter Dewin. What he could do, how he could help her, for what reason her faith was rested in him, she could not explain to herself. What would happen to her? What was the object of this senseless attack? . . .

Throughout the journey there had been one panic fear in her mind – that Leicester Crewe was responsible. She did not dare examine this possibility till now. Was that the explanation? Had she been asked to go to the theatre to give this man the opportunity he desired? . . .

He was not the kind who took risks. She knew his character well enough to understand that. He was capable of villainies, but they would be mean villainies – and this was one on the grand scale.

She looked at her watch; it was a quarter to one. And then she heard the sound of a key turning; the door opened slowly. Somebody was standing in the corridor outside – a figure of terror. From chin to heel it wore a tightly-fitting black coat. The face was concealed by a black bag drawn over the head. Level with the eyes an oblong piece of black tulle had been inserted so that the unknown could see without being seen.

He stood there for fully half a minute, looking at her, and then of a sudden he stepped back and the door closed gently. She heard the click of the lock, and that was all. Another ten minutes passed, and then the door opened again, and she braced herself to meet the dread figure; but this time it was another and stouter man, half his face hidden by a coloured handkerchief. She recognised in him her abductor.

'Do you know why you've been brought here, young lady?' he asked in a muffled tone.

She tried to speak, failed, and shook her head.

'You've been brought here because you're keeping company with people who are obnoxious to the Feathered Serpent.'

The man spoke slowly, as though he were remembering a message.

'If we like, we can keep you here for years, and nobody would be any the wiser. But if you'll give a solemn undertaking that you'll never reveal to a living soul what happened to you to-night, the Feathered Serpent will send you back unharmed.'

He waited for a reply. Again she tried to speak, and at the second attempt succeeded.

'I'll say nothing . . . of course. . . . I'll promise,' she said breathlessly.

It was not the moment to reproach him for her terrifying experience.

'You will speak to no living soul about to-night?'

'No . . . I – I promise!'

He went out of the cell, closed the door, and was gone some little time. When he returned he carried a tray, on which was a steaming cup of *bouillon*, a small roll and an unopened bottle of wine. She shook her head at the sight of the refreshment.

'No, thank you; I want water.'

'Better drink the soup,' he said, but went out, leaving the door open, to return with a glass of water, which she drank eagerly.

At his request she sipped at the *bouillon* and found it refreshing. When she had half finished it and put the cup aside:

'Are you ready?' he asked.

'Quite ready,' she answered. Her voice did not seem to be her own.

She followed him along the passage. The car was waiting at the door, and, to her great relief, he made no attempt to accompany her, but contented himself with a warning.

'If you're wise you'll sit quiet and make no attempt to attract attention. The police would not believe your story, anyway.'

The car did not go back the way it had come, but struck a new forest road, and she found herself returning to London by a route which was not familiar. Presently, with heartfelt gratitude, she saw certain familiar buildings of the City. . . . The clock was striking two as the car stopped before the doors of the silent block where she had her dwelling. She got down quickly, slammed the door behind her, and immediately the machine moved off.

She had the curiosity to look after it, but the number was so coated with mud as to be invisible. Daphne's hand was trembling so that she could hardly put the key in her door, and for an hour she lay fully dressed upon her bed, recovering gradually, and did not get up until her heart had ceased to beat so loudly that she almost heard the echo of it. When she did rise shakily to her feet and begin to undress, her knees trembled so that she had to hold on to the bed for support.

She thought she would not sleep that night, but hardly had she drawn the clothes over her shoulder before she fell into a dreamless slumber, from which she did not wake until at eleven o'clock the cleaner tapped at her door. She woke in consternation, and for the moment the knowledge that she was more than an hour late for work overshadowed the memory of that night of horror.

XV

'A young lady on the phone – she's phoned twice. I told her you were in bed and asleep,' said the cleaner, and with a start Daphne remembered Ella and her coat.

What explanation should she give to the girl? She went to the telephone and Ella's sharp voice hailed her.

'Whatever happened to you last night?' There were no 'my dears' this morning, Daphne noticed, but she was too bruised and weary to be amused.

'I got into the wrong car . . . it was waiting to take one of your company home, and I was out of London before I found that a mistake had been made.'

She was not a ready liar; her explanation sounded to her very halting. It sounded as if Miss Creed was not convinced.

'Are you sure that's what happened?' she asked, a note of suspicion in her voice. 'Somebody sent my chauffeur on a fool's errand. I thought they might have played a trick on you.'

'No, no, I assure you,' said Daphne in a panic.

Suppose Leicester Crewe was responsible for the outrage, this might be a trap to discover whether she was keeping her word.

'I'd like to see you to-day. Where will you be at two o'clock?'

She gave her Mr. Beale's address, and wondered whether the scientist would object to a visitor.

'Beale?' Ella was evidently writing down the name and address. 'All right; I'll call about two.'

Daphne hung up the telephone and went in search of an unappetising breakfast. It could not have been Leicester Crewe, unless he was using the name of the Feathered Serpent as a blind to cover his acts. And yet it fitted her conception of his character that he should weaken at the last moment in his infamous plan.

After breakfast she drove in a cab to Beale's house, and, meeting him in the hall, was full of apologies, which he cut short.

'I was rather worried about you,' he said. 'Please, please don't bother to explain. Any morning you feel like coming late, do so without the slightest misgiving.'

The old door was still leaning against the wall. Somebody had roughly cleaned it, and it was covered by queer arabesques drawn in charcoal.

'Do you notice the queer shape of that door?' He beamed on the unpromising object with the eye of an enthusiast. 'It is exactly the shape of an old Aztec doorway – I don't think their dwelling-houses had doors at all, as a matter of fact. Do you notice it is narrower at the top than at the bottom? That is not only a peculiarity of Aztec, but of old Egyptian architecture. I am satisfied in my mind, though many ethnologists disagree with me, that the Egyptians and the ancient South American Indians come from a common stock. . . .'

He was talking most of the morning, and it was rather difficult not to listen, though she felt the weariness of death. He noticed this just before lunch.

'You look terribly tired, Miss Olroyd,' he said. 'I hope you're not one of those young ladies who spend half the night dancing?'

Daphne smiled grimly.

'I certainly wasn't dancing last night,' she said, 'but I was out rather late.'

He did not question her, and she volunteered no explanation of a listlessness which continued throughtout the day.

Just before two came a telephone message from Ella. She was not able to call; would Daphne come to the theatre again that night? Daphne, whose last act before leaving her flat had been to send back the red coat by district messenger, answered emphatically that she had another engagement. She had a caller, however: Peter Dewin arrived at three o'clock. He had been out very early that morning and every minute had been fully occupied. She interviewed him in the drawing-room, and he was in his most buoyant mood.

'I've only to fit half a dozen more pieces into my jigsaw puzzle and it's complete,' he said. 'And what a story! Be enthusiastic!'

'Which story?' she asked, a little wearily, and he was quick to notice her unusual languor.

'Aren't you well?' he asked. 'You're as white as a sheet, and your eyes are like two burnt holes in a blanket!'

The one thing in the world about which she was unwilling to talk was herself, and she asked, a little brusquely for her:

'Have you come to see Mr. Beale?'

'I've come to see you,' he said emphatically. 'We are dining to-night at a very nice restaurant—'

'I am sleeping to-night,' she interrupted him, and his face fell. 'I'm terribly tired, and you would never forgive me if I went to sleep in the midst of your exciting conversation!'

'I could keep you awake with a whole lot of scandal,' he said enticingly.

'And I could tell you things that would make your hair stand on end,' she retorted, and they both laughed. 'Seriously, I'm much too tired to go out to-night.'

She stopped abruptly, and he had a feeling that she wanted to say something to him, and he was not far wrong; but though he waited, she said no more, but held out her hand.

'Are you going back to your Feathered Serpents—' he began, and was dumbfounded when she closed her eyes and shuddered.

'No, no, not Feathered Serpents,' she said. And then, hurriedly: 'Good-bye!'

She was gone before he could ask her a further question.

Whether she slept or woke, he must know the reason for this sudden antipathy to Feathered Serpents, and he resolved to be literally waiting on her doorstep when she came home that night. On his way he had called at Grosvenor Square, to find that Mr. Crewe was not only in the City, but had been there since nine o'clock. He had an office off St. Martin's le Grand – two small rooms at the very top of a high building. It was rather an address than a place he used, for he made very infrequent visits to the City, and one clerk was sufficient to deal with the business which trickled through this bureau.

He had been occupied since an early hour that morning, tabulating and pricing the stock which was held by the bank on his behalf. Mr. Leicester Crewe was unconscious of telepathic influence, but he had awakened that morning with the full intention of realising all his holdings and retiring to a place which was beyond the reach, and possibly beyond the knowledge, of the Feathered Serpent.

The Feathered Serpent was William Lane beyond question; and this ruthless William Lane, who killed without remorse, and whose menace was overshadowing three lives, was an altogether different individual from the silent man who had stood in the dock at the Old Bailey and had heard his sentence without a quiver of muscle.

Through the pleasant years that had passed, Crewe had almost forgotten that such a man as Lane existed; that in the silence of that grim prison set in the moorlands was one whom he had wronged as deeply as any man could wrong another.

Before his clerk arrived, Crewe had written a dozen letters of instructions to his brokers. It would take three or four days before he could draw money on his considerable holdings – it would have been easier to pledge them with the bank, but banks are shy of speculative shares, and on the whole it was better that he should sell out. He did not hold so much that his selling would have any important effect on the market, just then in a healthy condition.

Crewe was totalling his figures with an expression of satisfaction on his face, when the clerk brought in Peter's card. His first impulse was to refuse an interview; but he was as eager to receive news as Peter himself, and, clearing away the papers from his desk, he told the youth to admit the reporter.

'Sit down and have a cigar,' he said, laboriously genial. 'I can only give you five minutes: I'm rather busy just now. Well, what is the latest about the Feathered Serpent?'

His tone was flippant, but there was a suppressed apprehension in his voice. It was like a coward speaking lightly of death and quaking inwardly the while; and Peter Dewin saw here the cumulative effects of the terror which had fallen upon four people and had sent one flying the country and another to his grave.

'Nothing. You're giving evidence, I suppose, at the inquest?'

Crewe started.

'The inquest?' he stammered. 'Why – why, no; I'd forgotten there would be an inquest. Why should they want me?'

'Partly because you're the principal witness,' said Peter. 'I should have thought that you already would have been warned; and I'm wondering what the coroner will say when he knows that Mrs. Paula Staines has left the country in such a hurry.'

Crewe's jaw dropped, as he stared unbelievingly at the reporter.

'Left the country?' he repeated. 'What do you mean?'

'She left by the Flushing express this morning,' said Peter; 'and really, I don't blame her – I hope she has a happier crossing than her father had.'

His eyes were on Crewe as he spoke, and he saw the man's colour change from red to a dirty yellow.

'I didn't know her father,' he said shortly.

'Not the great Ricks?' mocked Peter.

The man was shaken. When he spoke his voice was shrill and husky.

'I don't know . . . Ricks. I always thought her name was Staines—' he began. 'I wish you wouldn't be so damned mysterious, Dewin.'

'Her name was Ricks – Paula Ricks. She was the daughter of Ricks, the forger, who shot himself a number of years ago. And nobody knows better than you, Mr. Crewe, that her name was Ricks.'

'She's left the country, you say? Are you sure?' Leicester avoided the implied reflection on his veracity.

'I saw her off,' said Peter. 'She didn't know, but I did! Somehow I had a feeling that she'd get away to-day, and I strolled down to watch two boat trains depart. She was on the first.'

'She may have gone across to Paris.'

Peter shook his head.

'Flushing is a long way round to Paris,' he said; 'even though her train connects with the Boulogne boat, her baggage went via Holland.'

Crewe was thinking quickly.

'I remember now, she said she was going away soon for a week—'

'She told the porter at Buckingham Gate that she was going away for a year,' said the calm Peter. 'No, you needn't have any illusions on the subject. Miss Ricks has gone definitely and finally, and I'm most anxious to know why one little word scared her out of the country.'

'One little word?'

Peter nodded.

'A queer little word – but it did the trick. I wonder if it would scare you?'

He was leaning on a chair, his arms resting on the back. Their eyes met.

'It'd take a pretty hefty word to scare me,' said Leicester Crewe steadily.

Peter had noticed a subtle change in the man. Before, when he had met him, he seemed a colourless, more or less uninteresting individual, with the manners, language and quasi-refinement of the successful business man who has been too preoccupied with his affairs to take up any more than the varnish of culture. In the past forty-eight hours the varnish had worn very thin, and a certain repellent ugliness of mind and manner showed beneath. He had coarsened; his voice had the harshness of a street hawker; from the deferential and polite resident of Grosvenor Square, he had reverted to the type from which he had developed.

'I'm going to talk to you plainly, young fellow,' he said. 'I've had all the mystery I want – do you get that? Some of you people are taking a liberty, and you're going to get hurt if you're not careful. I don't know who murdered Joe Farmer, but if your "little word" is anything to do with feathers or serpents, I'll tell you now that you're wasting your time. You can't scare me.'

'Mrs. Staines—' began Peter.

'To hell with Mrs. Staines!' he snarled. 'It doesn't matter two cents to me whether she's in the country or out! And I don't want to see anything you can show me,' he said violently, as Peter put his hand in his pocket and took out a letter.

Unabashed, the reporter extracted the sheet of paper it contained.

'This arrived at my lodgings by the first post this morning,' he said slowly. 'It is a typewritten document, and has no name or address.'

He laid the paper on the desk, twisting it round so that Leicester Crewe could see it, and the man read:

'LEICESTER CREWE (or Lewston):
    See London Sessions record under the name Lewston, Feb., 1905. Or Police Times issue, Feb. 14, 1905. Page 3, Col. 3.
'ELLA CREED. JOSEPH FARMER.
    See Marylebone police record June, 1910; also Paddington Times issue June 22nd, 1910. Name Farmster, née Lewston.'

'Well?' he said, looking up when he had finished.

'I've done a little quick research work this morning,' said Peter. 'Your name is Lewston. Miss Ella Creed is your sister. She was married to Farmster or Farmer when she was seventeen. You have been twice convicted, once for an insurance fraud, once for obtaining money by the sale of worthless shares. You escaped an earlier conviction for being concerned in the printing and distribution of forged Bank of England notes, through a technical error in the indictment. Your sister and Farmer were charged at

Marylebone Police Court with receiving stolen goods. You seem to be an enterprising family.'

Leicester Crewe licked his dry lips.

'What's the idea? Are you "putting the black" on me?'

Peter smiled.

'If that's a euphonious way of asking me whether I'm black-mailing you – I'm not!'

Crewe looked at the paper again, turned it over, held it up to the light.

'I don't care twopennorth of gin if all the world knows this about me,' he said harshly. 'I seem to remember a little bit of poetry about a man rising on his dead self to better things. It is no crime to get on in the world. And you won't get a penny out of me. You had better try Ella. I suppose the great idea is to produce this at the inquest and create one of your newspaper sensations?'

'It is not my idea,' said Peter softly. 'When I unearth a good story I like to have it entirely for myself. You may disabuse your mind of the illusion that you're being black-mailed. You're not. I'm trying to get the end of the real mystery, and I'm hoping that you'll give it to me.'

The man glowered at him.

'What real mystery?' he asked, and his voice was husky.

'The story of Gucumatz,' said Peter distinctly.

Not a muscle of Crewe's face moved, but from red it went to a deep purple, then to a waxy white again.

'Gucumatz!' he repeated mechanically.

He stared into the eyes of the reporter, and Peter saw his lips twist in a smile.

'What a fool I am! Of course, that word was in the purse. Joe Farmer carried it around with him, eh? It's the sort of fool thing he would do.'

Peter chuckled.

'Exactly the explanation which Mrs. Staines gave, and the right one!' he said, and added carefully: 'When I say "Staines" I mean "Ricks." She was rather amused and relieved, until—'

'Well?' asked the other, when he paused.

'Until I told her that Gucumatz is an Aztec word which means the Feathered Serpent.'

Crewe did not speak for a second, and then:

'How very interesting!' he drawled in his old Grosvenor Square manner.

He was master of himself; his poise was admirable. Yet Peter knew that this revelation had produced a shattering effect.

'Isn't everything too exciting?' Crewe went on, a faint smile hovering about his bloodless lips. 'Feathered Serpents . . .' he said slowly. 'So that's what it means, eh? That fellow is still alive?'

Peter nodded.

'William Lane is alive, yes: I don't think there's any doubt of that.'

Crewe sat down slowly and fiddled with the papers on his table.

'I wish I'd known,' he said; 'I'd have had him looked after from the moment he left prison.'

'What has he got on you?'

Crewe shook his head.

'You had better ask him when you see him – the police know that he killed poor old Joe? I suppose there's no – unwritten law in this country? A fellow can't go round shooting up people because . . . he's got a grudge against them, eh?'

He began turning over his papers again with an air of helpless futility.

'All right, Dewin. Thank you for the tip. I've got nothing to tell you. If you like to go along and squeak to your newspaper, by all means squeak; it won't worry me. So that's why Paula skipped, eh? I thought you were lying when you told me she'd gone, and yet I had a feeling, down in my mind, that it might be true. She called me a "quitter," and she's the first to quit! And Lane doesn't even know about her!'

'You wouldn't like to ease your mind and tell me how all this began?' asked Peter.

Mr. Crewe laughed hardly.

'I shouldn't like to stand in the dock of the Old Bailey and hear the old man say, "You'll go down for ten," should I? That's not my idea of passing the time. Do you want any money?' he asked, with brutal directness.

'I want all the money there is in the world,' said Peter quietly, 'but I don't want it from you, Crewe. You might save me a lot of trouble, and yourself too, if you let me in on this Gucumatz joke. Have you ever been to South America?'

For the first time during the interview Leicester Crewe seemed amused.

'I wouldn't know there was such a place if I hadn't got a block of tramway stock in Buenos Ayres. Do you know anybody who is likely to take it off my hands in a hurry?'

As he spoke, Peter had an inspiration.

'Why don't you see Mr. Beale – Mr. Gregory Beale? Somebody was telling me the other day that all his investments are in South American corporations.'

Leicester frowned.

'Beale . . .? Isn't that the fellow Daphne's working for?'

'He is the gentleman who employs Miss Olroyd,' said Peter.

Crewe shook his head.

'I don't know him; he's a pretty rich man, eh? What is the address?'

He scribbled it down on his blotting pad, and then:

'If a couple of hundred is any use to you, Dewin—'

'Get thee behind me,' said Peter. He stood in the doorway. 'But listen, Crewe – if your conscience gets busy, and you feel you'd like to unburden your soul to a reticent reporter, you'll find my number in the book.'

Peter owned a small car, which he had bought at third hand. It was not beautiful to look upon, but the engine never failed him. He might have got to Newbury by train, and taken a cab from there, but he preferred the open road and the solitude which gave him an opportunity of thinking.

His way led through Thatcham, and once he was clear of

Reading he began to keep a sharp look-out for the house which Hugg had burgled on the night of William Lane's death. There were quite a number which might possibly have been the scene of the burglary, and very wisely he stopped a cyclist policeman and inquired.

'Oh, yes, I remember the case,' said the officer. 'There was a tramp killed, a fellow named Lane. You'll find Mr. Bonny's house the third on the left from here, about a mile and a half along the road.'

Mr. Bonny was a fussy, rather excited man, who owned a number of grocers' shops in Berkshire, and he was very voluble on the subject of the outrage. A reporter must be a good listener, a skilful leader of irrelevant conversation into informative channels. It was a quarter of an hour before he began to talk news.

'. . . I saw the two rascals in the hall. From the landing outside my bedroom I could switch on the hall light, and I'd only to lean over the banisters to see them. The short, bald-headed man had the silver under his arm in a bag.' (Mentally Peter noted that Mr. Hugg had modestly omitted any mention of the silver, and had put the best interpretation upon his housebreaking exploit, namely that he was seeking clothing.) 'I saw the fellow who was killed – a tall, ugly-looking man—'

'But the man who was killed didn't break into the house, did he?' asked Peter quickly.

'Of course he did!' scoffed Mr. Bonny. 'He was the chap who threatened to murder me if I came down.'

He went on to describe rapidly his flight in the darkness, but Peter was not listening. The solution of this mystery was cleared up: the burglar who was killed was not William Lane, but Harry the Lag. William Lane was in the road outside, and was the only man who had escaped injury when Mr. Bonny's wildly driven motor-car had run them down in the road.

There was no reason why he should continue his inquiries any further. But to be absolutely sure, he went on first to Thatcham and then to Newbury and confirmed all that Mr. Bonny had told him.

Peter drove back to London in the gathering dark with the mystery of the ghostly taxi-driver explained. It was Harry the Lag who had been killed, and the third man, William Lane, had seized the opportunity that Bonny's absence in search of the police gave him, to slip into the dead man's pocket the papers which identified him as Lane. Apparently the police had made no attempt to investigate the identity of the dead man, but were satisfied to accept the evidence which they found in his jacket pocket. Had they taken his finger-prints, they would have known him at once for who he was. But why had William Lane taken this extraordinary step? For what reason did he wish to conceal his identity? Peter did not even ask himself this question for he knew beyond any shadow of doubt.

XVI

Whether Daphne Olroyd did or did not expect him to call, he could not discover from her manner. In truth, she could have fallen on his neck in gratitude, for the prospect of spending the evening alone was an appalling one. Her nerves were on edge, and she could hear noises, strange creakings and window-raisings which had no existence in fact. She had made a decision, and was within a few minutes of acting upon it when Peter called. He had a hint of her changed mood when she readily accepted his suggestion that they should go out to dinner – an invitation which he had anticipated would be declined.

He noticed that on a chair in the dining-room was a small suit-case, which was packed and strapped.

'Have you been or are you going?' he asked.

'I'm going,' she said calmly, and to his surprise: 'If you had come half an hour later I shouldn't have been here – I have taken a room for a week at the Ridley Hotel. It is Bloomsbury and cheap, but it is very comfortable, and I know a woman who is staying there.'

'But why on earth?' he asked. 'Have you let your flat or is the roof leaking?'

She shook her head.

'You're frightened!'

She flushed at this.

'Why should I be?' she asked indignantly.

Peter scratched his chin and looked at the girl long and thoughtfully.

'There's no reason why you should be,' he said slowly, 'and I wish you weren't – I suppose that murder has got right on top of you? What a brute I am! I never thought of that.'

She made an attempt to treat the matter casually, but he was not deceived.

'I don't know why I have decided to try an hotel,' she said vaguely. 'I was sitting here wondering what I should do with the evening, and – the flat got on my nerves, so I rang up the hotel and asked them to let me have a room. You think I'm silly?'

'I think you're wise,' he said quietly. 'Not that there is the slightest danger to you—'

The telephone bell rang at that moment.

'You can do me a great favour,' she said, in a low voice, as though she feared to be overheard. 'Would you answer that? I think it is Miss Creed. She wants me to come to her to-night, and I told her I was going out to dinner with – with—'

'With me,' said Peter. 'How providential!'

He lifted up the receiver; but it was not Ella Creed's voice which greeted him. A deep, masculine voice, evidently disguised, spoke to him.

'Is that Miss Olroyd?'

It was a loud, spluttering telephone, and Peter answered in a low tone: 'Yes.' He had no intention of deceiving the person at the other end. The dropping of his voice was almost mechanical to attune to a very sensitive instrument.

'You remember?' said the voice. 'You are to tell nobody of what happened last night!'

There was a click, and silence. Peter hung up the receiver slowly and looked at the girl.

'Who was it?' she asked.

'What happened to you last night?' he demanded, and saw the alarm in her eyes.

'Nothing,' she said defiantly, 'nothing that I can tell.'

'Nothing that you can tell Tom or Dick or Harry, but something you can tell Peter,' he said steadily. 'What was it?'

'Who was it speaking?' she asked.

She was breathless, terrified. To his consternation he saw that she was trembling from head to foot.

'You've got to tell me, Daphne,' he said gently. 'Something happened to you last night – I'm a fool or I'd have known that this morning when I saw you. What was it?'

She shook her head, but there was no emphasis in the gesture.

'I can't tell you – I promised. I really can't tell you.'

He took her by the shoulders and looked down into her eyes.

'I'm not asking you to tell me because I want news – something to print,' he said in a low voice. 'I want you to tell me because I – I am fond of you, Daphne.'

She looked up at him quickly, and as quickly withdrew her eyes. The pink came back to her face, only to fade again, but she did not answer. He shook her gently.

'Tell me.'

'I oughtn't – I promised,' she said haltingly. 'Somebody took me from the theatre . . .'

And then, incoherently, she told the story of her night's adventure, and every word she spoke brought her relief.

'. . . They didn't hurt me – nobody touched me. They were rather – kind. And Peter, you're not to say a word about this – do you hear, not a word! And you mustn't try to find the place.'

And then, to her own amazement, she burst into tears and lay sobbing on his breast. It was a long time before she was calm again.

'I'm hysterical, I suppose, but it's been a dreadful thing to keep in my own mind, without help or advice,' she said, when she had bathed her face, and removed some of the evidence of her distress by a process which Peter did not attempt to analyse. 'It was horrible, wasn't it? And I've done nothing to anybody!'

The arm that encircled her squeezed her a little.

'Of course you haven't, my dear. And the moment they found you'd done harm to none, they let you go. Don't you see that?'

'But why? How?' she asked, bewildered.

'They thought you were Ella: that is why they carried you off. You wore her red coat; and I happen to know that Ella always wears a red coat – it's one of her advertising schemes. The moment the Feathered Serpent got you to his little lair—'

'The Feathered Serpent?' she breathed. 'Was it he?'

Peter nodded.

'Of course it was. The moment he found you weren't Ella, he sent you home again. Like a prison cell, was it?'

'It was terrible!' She shivered.

'That was the plot,' he mused; 'to put Ella in a little prison that he'd built for her, and to keep her there for years and years and years. He's probably got a prison routine all mapped out for her.'

'But why?' protested Daphne.

'Because, in some way I haven't discovered yet, Gucumatz was put into prison—'

'Who is Gucumatz?' she asked in surprise. 'I've never heard his name before.'

'He's a particular friend of mine,' said Peter glibly. 'He was put into prison, not on the evidence, but through Ella Creed. I spent all last night reading up the particulars of the Lane case, and Ella certainly did not appear in court; in fact, the only member of the gang that was present was Joe Farmer.'

'You're puzzling me dreadfully,' she interrupted. 'I don't know what you're talking about. Was Mr. Farmer prosecuting this man with the strange name?'

'Let's go to dinner,' said Peter, and to his own surprise he lifted her face to his and kissed her. Daphne did not seem greatly distressed.

He picked up her suitcase, and, as they were going:

'Do you think I'm being very silly?' she asked.

He shook his head.

'I think you're rather wise,' he said. 'The Feathered Serpent is not the only bird of prey who is on the wing to-night.'

As they came out of the flat, he saw a man standing on the edge of the pavement, and his figure was familiar. As the cab he summoned slowed up at the kerb, he put the girl and the suit-case inside, and walked towards the lounger.

'Do you want me, Hugg?' he asked.

'Yes, sir.' The little convict's voice was hoarse with emotion. 'I've seen him again to-night.'

'William Lane?'

'Yes, sir.'

Peter thought for a moment as a suspicion crossed his mind.

'How did you know I was here?' he asked.

'I went round to your house to see you, and you wasn't in. Then I went round to Grosvenor Square to see Mr. Crewe, and he wasn't in either, and I asked where his secretary was, and they told me that she'd left. They gave me her address, and I was coming here to find out if she knew where—'

'Why should she?' asked Peter. And then, in a sudden change of tone: 'Well, where did you see William Lane?'

'In a Rowton House. He's a sick man, nearly dead. He borrowed five shillings off me to get to Birmingham, where he's got some relations.'

Hugg talked in a nervous, jerky way which was not like him. He could not keep still, but shuffled from one foot to the other. Peter could have sworn that his teeth were chattering.

'I see,' he said. 'Come to the office to-morrow morning and ask for me – eleven o'clock sharp.'

'Yes, sir.'

Again that eagerness, that nervous intensity which seemed so foreign to this usually phlegmatic crook.

Peter walked back to the cab, jumped in and slammed the door behind him.

'An old friend of mine,' he said easily, and made no reference to the conversation.

In the middle of dinner he left the restaurant and called up Leicester Crewe.

'I can't talk on the telephone,' said Crewe pettishly, when he discovered who the caller was. 'If you want to see me, come round to-night – now, if you like.'

'Did you get into touch with the person I suggested might buy your shares?' asked Peter, and in a milder tone the man answered that he had. He added a reluctant expression of thanks for the information which the reporter had supplied. 'I think I can do a deal with him; I've been talking to him on the telephone, and I'm seeing him to-morrow night.'

Peter came back to the girl, and was in his gayest mood for the rest of the evening. He had chosen the little restaurant of the hotel where she had her lodgings, and he left her soon after half-past nine and hurried back to the office to gather and edit all the outside news that had come concerning the killing of Farmer. The date of the inquest had been fixed for the following Tuesday, and he found amongst his letters one from Clarke, asking him to call at his convenience at Scotland Yard.

Sitting down at his typewriter, he rattled off the best part of a column, and the night editor read it through without enthusiasm.

'There's very little meat in this. Didn't you get a new line to-day? – all this stuff has been in the evening papers, and most of it you've pinched from the agencies.'

'In spite of my unconscious plagiarism,' said Peter, 'it reads to me like a pretty good column.'

With his nose on the trail of a crime story, Peter Dewin was indefatigable. Midnight found him in the frowsy atmosphere of Victoria Dock Road; and here he had the good fortune to find a local detective sergeant who knew him, and had been in the district off and on for years.

'What were you after? I saw you speaking to the oldest inhabitant of Wormwood Scrubs,' said the sergeant when Peter joined him. 'Are you getting local colour, or are you on a story?'

'I'm on the Farmer murder,' he said, and the officer expressed his understanding.

'He had a public-house here in the old days, the "Rose and Crown." I'm pretty certain he used it as a blind to carry on an extensive fencing business.'

'Was he married in those days?'

The sergeant shook his head.

'He never had a wife here, though he was very friendly with one or two girls.'

Peter mentioned the name of the Lewstons without awakening any response.

'Never heard of them,' said the sergeant.

They were pacing up a long, dingy street, and the sergeant stopped and pointed.

'There's the "Rose and Crown."'

It was a tiny, mean-looking public-house, its windows dark, and stood at the corner of a side street.

'Farmer used to live there. In fact, this is becoming quite a show place,' he said humorously. 'We had the biggest "slush" raid that's ever been carried out in this district, at the end house.'

'William Lane?' suggested Peter.

'Oh, you remember the case, do you? Yes, Lane. We caught him with the goods, plant, photographic apparatus, machines for printing, and about a thousand *mille* notes ready for export. Somebody gave us the office, and Sweeney came down from Scotland Yard. We raided it at eleven o'clock at night and caught Lane red-handed, as you might say. I forget whether he got seven or ten years. Farmer was the principal witness against him.'

'Can you tell me anything about Lane?'

The sergeant shook his head as they slowly walked towards the house of tragedy.

'No. He'd been living there for three or four weeks before we raided the house. None of the neighbours knew him. He never went out till late at night. In those days his kitchen used to lead to a narrow lane between the backs of the houses in Manting Street, and it was supposed that he got his machinery and plant in by the back way. The only thing he said when he was arrested was: "I alone am responsible." I don't think he spoke another word. He wasn't even defended by counsel till the judge ordered a young lawyer to stand up for him.'

He knew nothing whatever about Crewe, either in his own or his assumed name.

'It's difficult to keep track of 'em. This used to be the head-quarters of about six of the biggest gangs in London, and they were swell gangs too! There's been more cocaine brought into this area than into Limehouse; more stolen motor-cars shipped from here than honest machines from Southampton!'

Of the Feathered Serpent he had never heard till he had read in the morning newspaper about Farmer's murder.

'It's a queer case. My own theory is that somebody he shopped is getting back on him.' And, as a thought struck him, he uttered an exclamation. 'I wonder if it's Lane? He was due out last summer, and he's got reason enough for wanting to get even with Joe!'

Peter's investigations were not completed after he had left the police officer, and it was not until three o'clock in the morning that he dragged himself wearily up the stairs of his boarding house, so tired that he could hardly summon energy to undress.

He was in that condition which he would describe as being 'over-tired' – meaning no more than that his brain had drawn a new stimulus from his over-burdened body and mocked physical exhaustion with mental activity which prohibited sleep.

XVII

He had had problems equally insoluble, but they had never before kept him awake at night. He dozed heavily and wakened, twisted growlingly in his bed, and was on the point of sleeping when again he wakened. He thought he had heard a noise outside his window.

He got out of bed, threw up the lower sash of the window and looked out. It was a clear, cold night of stars, and he was looking down into the small garden at the back of the house. 'Garden' was a complimentary term for a grass-grown square of microscopic size, with a narrow flower bed running under the walls. He found it more than a little chilly, dressed as he was in his thin sleeping suit, and he was on the point of withdrawal when he saw, or imagined he saw, a figure glide from the shadow of the wall, cross the tiny lawn and disappear into the gloomy shade of the opposite wall.

He leaned farther out, peering into the darkness, and as he stretched out his hand to balance himself on the sill, he touched something cold. It was a steel hook, except that there was no sharp point at the end, but instead a circle of rubber. He tried to draw it to him, but it was fastened, and he understood why. The stout rubber must have been fashioned in the shape of a hollow cup which formed a vacuum, so that when the end of the hook touched the steel it was impossible that it could slip. With his fingers he prised up the edge of the 'sucker' and drew the hook and its attachment into the room. He found it was a hook-ladder made of light but strong bamboo, about ten feet in length; so long, in fact, that he had a difficulty in manœuvring it into his bedroom.

Fortunately he had not put on the light, and as soon as the ladder was drawn in, he stepped softly to the mantelpiece, found the electric hand-lamp which he kept for emergencies, and, slipping into his dressing gown, tiptoed back to the open window and sent a white ray of light into the restricted area of the back yard.

There was nothing to be seen, but it was quite possible that the intruder was well hidden by the small bicycle house which had been erected by his landlady along one wall, for it was in this direction that he had seen the figure move.

There were several ways by which the intruder might have got into the back yard. Running the length of the short street in which his lodgings were situated was a broad wall which divided the houses from those that backed on to them, and the burglars, if burglars they were, could easily have come that way; or they might have taken the simpler method of surmounting the wall from which the earlier intruder had dropped; for, like Mr. Beale's house, the lodging was built on a corner lot.

Peter sent the light down the wall carefully, and presently he saw another hook ladder hanging from yet another window-sill.

'Mysteriouser and mysteriouser!' he muttered, and, closing down the window, he dressed hurriedly in the dark. All traces of weariness had left him. The overmastering desire for sleep had been replaced by a slight buzzing in his head, which was nature's warning that he had very nearly reached the end of his physical tether.

Five minutes later he was out of the house, carrying a lamp in one hand and a walking stick in the other. As he turned the corner, he saw a man drop from the wall, and challenged him. For a second the figure stood as though about to answer, and then, turning, he ran with the dash of a sprinter across the road, with Peter in pursuit. And then, when it seemed that he must escape, there appeared from nowhere a helmeted shape. A beam of light smote the runner in the eyes and blinded him, and a firm hand gripped him by the collar and swung him to the ground. There was a brief struggle, and then Peter came up.

'All right,' said a surly voice, 'it's a cop!'

Legally no policeman has the right to 'fan' a prisoner until he gets into the police station; but the policeman was on the side of caution. There had been a number of armed burglaries in Kensington, and it was not until he had satisfied himself that the man was carrying nothing more lethal than a small jemmy, that he marched him to the station, Peter gripping one arm and the constable the other.

'Are you the feller I was after?' said the man as they were nearing the police station. 'Name of Dewin?'

'I am the victim,' said Peter cheerfully.

'I don't know how you heard me.'

In the man's voice was a note of despair that one might have expected to hear in a disappointed artist who for some unaccountable reason had found his picture rejected by the Academy.

'I never made a sound! This "flattie" don't know me, but the inspector will.'

'Not so much of the "flattie,"' said the indignant policeman thus labelled. 'I knew you as soon as I saw your ugly face – you're Lightfoot Jerry.'

The prisoner made a clucking sound of wonder.

'Fancy a "flattie" knowing anything!' he said.

'I was at the West London police court the last time you were charged,' said the officer with satisfaction. 'I never forget faces.'

'Marvellous!' said the sarcastic Jerry.

In the light of the charge-room the local detective inspector, who happened to be on duty at the moment, hailed Jerry as an old friend; yet his greeting was not cordial.

'Working on my manor, Jerry!' he said reproachfully. 'You're taking a liberty if ever a man took one!'

It is one of the peculiar and unwritten laws of the underworld that no known felon shall commit a crime in the district where he resides. As a reward for this abstention he has the privilege of residence without undue interference by the police. He is, so to speak, a guest in the house of the divisional inspector; he is more or less free from police observation, and he is not liable at any moment to be pulled in as a suspicious person under the Prevention of Crimes Act. Officially, of course, there is no such arrangement or understanding, but actually, the professional thief goes abroad into other districts to commit his offences against the law, and avoids fouling his own nest.

'I'm very sorry, Mr. Brown,' said Jerry humbly. 'But I was getting a hundred quid for this job, and everything found for me, and I couldn't turn him down.'

'The usual "madam"!' sneered the inspector.

'It's not "madam," Mr. Brown,' said Jerry earnestly, 'though I admit it sounds as likely as cream in skilly; but it's true.'

Then and there Lightfoot Jerry told an extraordinary story. On the previous morning about twelve o'clock he had received a pencilled note, asking him if he'd like to do a job and promising him a hundred pounds. If he agreed, he was to take the note at six o'clock in the evening to the place where the railway bridge crosses the Great West Road. Under the bridge his employer would be waiting for him, to give instructions. The hour chosen was one when pedestrians on the Great West Road are fewer than they are in the day time, for the West Road is essentially a motor speedway.

There were enclosed with the note two Treasury notes, each for a pound, as earnest, and whilst suspecting a police trap, for Jerry shared with all thieves the illusion that the police have no other occupation in life than to arrange pitfalls for the unlawful, he kept the appointment.

The road was absolutely deserted, but when he reached the railway arch a car drove up to the kerb and a man got out.

'I couldn't see his face, and I couldn't recognise him again if you gave me ten thousand pounds,' he said frankly. 'He told me the job he wanted me to do, and said that the ladders would be put over the wall ready for me. He gave me a plan of the house, and where this gentleman's room was to be found, and all I had to do was to find a purse and a key which he kept under his pillow.'

'With a million sterling in it?' asked the inspector sardonically.

'It had a key in it – that's all I know,' insisted the man. 'And listen, inspector! You think this is a cock and bull story, but there's a Big Fellow in London who's using us old lags and paying well. The only thing I know is that he drives a taxi sometimes.'

He was dogged on this point, that the metropolis held a generous employer of ex-convicts, who seemed to know the right man for the right job. He would not mention the names of any men who had been so engaged.

Peter drew the sceptical inspector aside.

'I think you ought to get on to Clarke about this bird,' he said seriously. 'I'm perfectly sure that it is a Feathered Serpent crime.'

The inspector nodded.

'I've known Lightfoot for years—'

He hesitated. The name of Chief Inspector Clarke was one to conjure with. He had in fact been promoted to Superintendent that very morning, and was actually in charge of the area. There are four big men at headquarters, each of whom is in charge of one section of London, with a superintendent controlling the 'four great manors.' It was to the latter position that the inspector had been promoted.

He went into his little office and Peter heard him telephoning. In five minutes he came back.

'Mr. Clarke's coming down to see this man,' he said, in a more serious tone. 'He seems to think you're right, that the Big Fellow Jerry spoke about is the Feathered Serpent.'

And then a thought occurred to Peter, and he asked to be allowed to question the man, but here he found the inspector adamant. Jerry had been taken to a cell, and it was not until the arrival of Clarke, an hour later, that Peter was able to put his question.

The prisoner had been aroused from his sleep and brought up to the inspector's office. He was naturally in a bad humour, resenting more this interruption to his slumber than his arrest.

'You've been inside, Jerry, haven't you?' asked Peter, and when the man had sulkily agreed: 'Did you know a man named William Lane?'

Lightfoot Jerry considered.

'Yes, I've seen him in Dartmoor; he was in D Ward, I was in A – he was in for printing slush.'

'Did you ever talk to him?'

Jerry shook his head.

'Never spoke to him in my life. He used to work in the shoemaker's shop with Harry the Lag and little Hugg, the burglar. He was in hospital while I was there, but I was in one of the downstairs cells, and I never had a chance of speaking to him.'

'Do you think he was the man you met by appointment under the railway arch?' asked Peter, and the ex-convict thought.

'No . . . and yet it might have been. I never heard Lane speak, and from what I have been told he didn't speak much. I saw him in church once or twice and in the shoe-making shop, but most of my time I was in the bake-house or the laundry.'

After the man had been taken back to his cell, Clarke, who had been very silent during the questioning, took Peter by the arm and led him out into the street.

'What was he after, that fellow?'

Peter knew that it was not the moment to be mysterious.

'He was after a key and a cryptogram,' he said, and putting his hand in his pocket, took out the purse. 'I won't tell you how it came into my possession, because another person is involved, but this key was carried about by Joe Farmer, and I don't think you'd have been much wiser even if you'd had it.'

They went back into the police station and Clarke examined the paper.

'"Gucumatz" is the word. It's an old Aztec word meaning "Feathered Serpent." The key is a little baffling. If I knew what that signified, there would not be any Feathered Serpent mystery. As it is, I'm just as far off understanding as I have ever been.'

Clarke turned the key over and over on the palm of his hand; tried with the aid of a magnifying glass to decipher the obliterated letters, but confessed himself baffled.

'Have you any theory?' he asked.

Peter shook his head.

'This case is moving in such an atmosphere of melodrama that I should not feel I was being very romantic if I put forward the suggestion that it is the key of a box containing important papers. My mind, however, is in revolt against any such theory.'

'It looks to me more like the key of a door, except that it is a little small for that.'

Clarke put away the key in the purse and slipped it into an inside pocket.

'You know a great deal more about this case than you've told me, Dewin,' he said, 'but I think if I discover the door that is opened by this key, I shall have beaten you out of sight!'

It was past five o'clock when Peter got home, and he decided that the last thing in the world he wanted to do was to go to bed. He had a bath and shaved, and then made the fatal mistake of lying down half dressed under his eiderdown for a brief rest. . . . It was the clanging of the luncheon gong that woke him.

XVIII

It needs a touch of the bizarre to waken thoroughly the interest of any great city, either in an individual or in an act. It was just the hint of gruesome mystery that the Feathered Serpent supplied, which raised the Farmer murder from a commonplace, if somewhat interesting, item of crime news to the importance it afterwards assumed.

It took little over twenty-four hours for London to appreciate the uncomfortable fact that somewhere in its midst was a secret organisation, ruthless in its methods, diabolically cunning in its plans, and though newspapers could hint, without allowing plainness of speech to approach the borderline of libel, that the Feathered Serpent was concerned with dealing vengeance on a very few members of the community, it happened that one of those few was a popular musical comedy actress, and when this was known a new value was added to the story.

Peter went to the office to find the news editor interviewing the ex-convict Hugg; and the first thing that struck Peter on seeing the little man was his extraordinarily prosperous appearance. He wore a smart suit of clothes, his collar and linen were shiningly new. He had indulged himself in the luxury of a shave, and carried a furled umbrella hooked on to his arm.

'Oh, here you are, Dewin! This man was very anxious to see somebody in connection with the Feathered Serpent story. He says he told you that he had seen a man named Lane driving a cab—'

'It wasn't him at all, Mr. Dewin,' broke in Hugg rapidly. 'I've seen the feller that I thought was Lane, stopped him in the Strand to-day, and I'm blest if it wasn't somebody else altogether! This is a warning to me, Mr. Dewin. I'd had a couple of drinks that night, and naturally I was a bit bat-eyed. So I went up to this feller and I said: "Is your name Lane?" but I'd no sooner had a good look at him than I knew I was wrong.'

'Come here,' said Peter sternly, took the little man firmly by the arm and led him into a small editorial waiting-room. 'Now, you perjuring villain,' he said good-naturedly, 'what is this stuff you're trying to get across the footlights of life?'

'It's true – if I drop dead this minute—' began Hugg.

'Listen!' Peter dug his forefinger in the man's chest to emphasise his every point. 'Yesterday I found you waiting outside a certain block of flats to tell me that you had seen William Lane; he was very ill and he was going off to Birmingham, and that you lent him—'

'Yes, that's right, Mr. Dewin,' said Hugg eagerly. 'That was William Lane all right. He left London—'

Peter interrupted him with a raised hand.

'You've seen William Lane: I don't doubt that,' he said, 'and he's threatened you that unless you carried a story to the police that he's left London, he'll do something very unpleasant. That is why you came to find me. He told you that I'd very likely be somewhere near Miss Olroyd's lodgings. Wait,' he said, as Hugg began an incoherent explanation. 'He saw you again subsequent to this, questioned you as to what you told me, learnt about the taxicab story, and has sent you on to eat your words. He probably gave you the money to dress yourself decently, and that is why you're looking like a Bond Street fashion plate. Well?'

Hugg did not reply. His shifty eyes looked everywhere but at Peter.

'I've got my living to get,' he said vaguely. 'It's not my job to go squeaking to the police or to reporters. If a man makes a mistake when he's intoxicated, why shouldn't he come and own up?'

'Where did you see Lane?' asked Peter, ignoring the question, but Hugg was less inclined to talk than ever.

'Let up on this feller,' he almost pleaded. 'He's got his own graft, and it's not for me to try and trip him up. Take my advice, Mr. Dewin. He's a pretty bad feller, this whoever he is.'

'Have you seen Lane?'

Hugg shook his head, and then, to Peter's surprise, tiptoed to the door and listened.

'You never know where that bird will be,' he said fretfully, and, lowering his voice: 'I haven't seen him, and that's a fact. I got a note telling me to be at a certain place and he'd come along. It was in a little country road just north of Barnet. I went there and he come up in a car – he didn't leave the car, but talked to me through the window. It was one of these shut-in affairs, and there was nobody in it but himself.'

'A saloon?' suggested Peter.

'I don't know what you call it. I didn't see his face, I tell you. All that he said to me was—' he swallowed something and shivered – 'that I had to go and see you and tell you I'd made a mistake. He said he didn't want any innocent person suspected. They were his very words, Mr. Dewin – he didn't want an innocent person suspected.'

'Was it Lane's voice?' asked Peter.

Hugg shook his head.

'I couldn't swear to it. I think he had a mask or something, but I couldn't see his face. And then he told me where I'd find you, and what I was to tell you, I had to report to him again that night, but in a different place. It might be Lane. There's several people who had a down on Joe Farmer. In fact I've heard fellers in Dartmoor say that if ever they got the chance they'd "out" him. He told me I was to keep myself respectably dressed, that he might want me at any time – I've gone into lodgings at Lambeth.'

'That's a lie,' said Peter – he had an extraordinary and uncanny instinct for untruths.

'It's as near to the truth as you'll ever get from me,' said Mr. Hugg paradoxically.

Mr. Hugg retired on that line. The hall porter told Peter that he had left a new suitcase in the hall and went off in a cab. Evidently he did not find London a healthy place.

Peter stopped long enough at the office to check up the items of news about the case which the agencies had turned in, and then went out to make a call at Scotland Yard.

Mr. Gregory Beale's house was one of those smooth-working establishments that seem to be run by clockwork. His servants were men and women past middle age, who had been in his employ for years; and for the first time in her life Daphne Olroyd learnt what perfect service could be. Of the taciturn butler she saw very little, and it was from the cook, a stout and elderly woman, that she learnt something of the interior economy of the house.

Wednesday was the servants' holiday, she discovered. Mr. Beale dined out at night, had the front door bell switched through to his study, so that he himself answered the door if occasion demanded, and on one occasion had prepared his own luncheon.

'But that was too much of a bother to him – after that he kept me until three in the afternoon.'

His servants adored him, with every reason, for he was the most generous and humane of employers, and if his consideration for their comfort sometimes approached the realms of eccentricity, it was a lovable trait in him.

It was on Wednesday morning, and Daphne was deep in her new work of classification. The big front drawing-room had been converted for the moment into a museum. Most of the chairs and tables had been removed and down two sides of the handsome room ran long, bare, wooden tables, covered now with a heap of curios awaiting her attention.

With the help of a little book which he had found for her, she was able to make a rough catalogue without his assistance, and only occasionally did she carry some weird piece of pottery or some strange flint knife to the study to get his help. Occasionally he wandered aimlessly into the room, his hands in his pockets, a smile upon his eager face, and would hold forth in his oracular manner and she would be spellbound. Sometimes it was on the most mundane subjects; occasionally he dealt with Aztec civilisation, and then he was most interesting.

'Seventy-five different varieties of the Feathered Serpent have been discovered,' he told her that morning. 'And I don't know how many legends there are – every district has its own. I have found traces of Feathered Serpent worship in Peru.'

There were half a dozen models of this queer god and he took one up and examined it with a curious smile.

'Your friend has rather spread himself on the subject of Feathered Serpents this morning,' he said. 'Have you seen the *Post-Courier*?'

She had not had time to read the newspaper.

He shook his head distastefully.

'I asked him not to use my name, but unfortunately—'

'He didn't break his word?' asked Daphne quickly, and Mr. Beale laughed.

'No, the fault was entirely mine. He used a photograph of the Feathered Serpent, one that I gave him. Unhappily I have the copyright of these photographs, and I suppose that the printers, seeing "Copyrighted by Gregory Beale" written on the back, thought it was an act of courtesy to reproduce my name under the picture. It can't be helped, and it really isn't at all important.'

She wanted very badly to tell him of her adventure in Epping Forest, but the memory of the warning that Peter had received over the telephone inhibited the confidence.

'Obviously,' he went on, 'this man Farmer must have offended somebody very badly. I was reading the case at breakfast, and it struck me that he must have been, at some period of his life, a criminal or an associate of criminals.'

'Why do you say that?' she asked in surprise.

He shrugged his shoulders.

'It is a theory of mine,' he said.

It was now that he too told her his practice of giving Wednesday off to his two men-servants.

'You have a very good view of the front of the house, Miss Olroyd,' he said. 'Perhaps if you saw anybody coming up the steps who did not receive an immediate reply from me, you would not mind opening to him? – I get so absorbed in my work that I do not even hear bells ring!'

The particular work in which he was so enthusiastically engaged was, he told her, the compilation of a new series of folklore stories which he had gathered in Central America. Evidently they contained either something unusually startling, or else material which he did not think desirable should be read by his young secretary, for he kept the manuscript locked away in his safe, and she had an idea that it was put away sheet by sheet as he wrote it. She was too interested in her own work to have much time for looking out of the window, and three times after lunch she heard him go to the door, and on the third occasion went out to speak to him.

'I'm so sorry, Mr. Beale,' she said penitently, 'but I will keep a better look out. You ought really not to answer the door if I'm in the house.'

He chuckled at this, and seemed pleased.

'Your absorption is a very good sign,' he said. 'You're taking an intelligent interest in Feathered Serpents, and in the near future I can imagine that you will be interviewed by enterprising news-paper reporters on the subject of these strange beasts.'

Thereafter Daphne pulled her table to the centre of the room, and sat so that she commanded a view of the street. The fourth caller she saw before the little coupé stopped and Ella Creed alighted.

Ella Creed! Then Daphne remembered that the woman had promised to call – was it yesterday or the day before, or an eternity ago? She hurried out into the hall. Here was a caller to entertain whom Gregory Beale would not wish to be taken from his work.

Ella greeted her with a stiff nod.

'Oh, you're here, are you? It's a devil of a place to find,' she said.

She turned to her chauffeur and gave him an order in her high, shrill voice, and the car moved on.

'He's got to go and pick up some dresses for me,' she said, 'and I can go back by taxi.'

Daphne offered no apology when she led her visitor into the untidy drawing-room, and removing a dust-sheet from one of the chairs, pushed it towards her.

'What are you doing?' asked Ella, frowning round.

It was characteristic of her that her first glimpse was one of appraisal.

'This fellow's got plenty of money,' she said, pointing to a picture over the mantelpiece. 'That's a Gainsborough.'

Daphne was surprised and a little puzzled to learn that the actress had a knowledge of art, and, as though she read her thoughts, the woman continued:

'I know a lot about pictures – their selling value anyway. I have a boy friend – one of the Lecksteins, the art dealers, and he's given me lots of tips. What is all this stuff?' She waved a hand disparagingly at the laden tables.

Daphne explained, and the woman's nose wrinkled a little contemptuously.

'It doesn't look worth the trouble of collecting.' And then, abruptly: 'Where did you go the other night?'

For the moment Daphne was nonplussed. Even now she had not succeeded in finding an alternative explanation if that which she had already given was unconvincing, as apparently it was.

'All that stuff about being driven in the wrong car and not finding where you were till too late, is bunk!' said Ella. 'You needn't think up any lies, because I know it is. Somebody mistook you for me, didn't they?'

Daphne nodded.

'I thought so!' And, after a pause: 'Well, aren't you going to tell me what happened?'

'I'm afraid I can't – I promised.'

The woman was looking at her intently, as though she sought to probe the secret that lay behind Daphne Olroyd's eyes.

'You didn't tell the police, or anything? You're a fool! If it had been me, no promise would have counted, you bet your life!'

Daphne could not help thinking that had her unknown captors taken the woman they sought, no promise would have been necessary.

In the cold light of day Ella's face was a little haggard. She had made up carelessly, and there was a certain coarseness about her features which Daphne had not observed before.

'This thing's getting on my nerves,' she said. 'What did Dewin say? You and he are very thick, aren't you? Does he believe – but I don't suppose he discusses the matter with you.'

Ella walked across to the table and picked up one of the little models.

'Beale likes this sort of thing, doesn't he? I saw in the paper that he knows all about Feathered Serpents – what are they?'

'That is one you're holding,' said Daphne, and the woman started and nearly dropped the fragile thing.

'Good God! Is it?' She looked at the clay figure with a new interest, and at that moment, looking past her, Daphne saw a man walking up the steps: a tall, cadaverous-looking man, seedily dressed. She was about to excuse herself and go out to find his business, when through the half-open door of the drawing-room she heard Mr. Beale's quick step in the hall.

'Feathered Serpent, eh?' said Ella thoughtfully, twisting the object round and round in her hand. 'That doesn't look very terrible, does it?'

Beale was talking to somebody, and his voice was unusually sharp.

'Feathered—' began Ella again.

And then Daphne heard a queer choking sound and turned. For a moment she was paralysed with amazement. The actress was staring at the clay thing in her hand with wide, distended eyes. Her face under the rouge had gone white and old. . . .

Daphne had time to reach her before she collapsed. She heard the slam of the front door and ran out into the hall.

'Miss Creed . . . she's fainted or something,' she said incoherently.

'Miss Creed?' He stared at her over his glasses. 'She's the actress—'

'Can't you help me, please?' said Daphne desperately.

He pushed past her into the room, took one glimpse at the figure, then, stooping, lifted her without an effort.

'I'll take her into my study,' he said. 'Get a glass of water; and go upstairs to my room – you'll find a medicine chest in the bathroom. There's a bottle of sal volatile: bring it down.'

She returned in a few minutes to find him forcing water from a wineglass between the lips of the half-conscious woman.

'Your medicine chest—' she began.

'I know, I know.' He was almost short with her. 'It was in my study all the time. I forgot that I had brought it down. I think she will be all right very soon. These cases make a quick recovery. What happened?'

Daphne told him of the Feathered Serpent, and following his glance at the table, she saw the figure was there.

'It was clasped in her hand when I brought her in,' he said. 'What an odd coincidence!'

Daphne looked anxiously down at the girl. She was breathing regularly, but was still unconscious.

'I should imagine it is a heart attack,' said Mr. Beale, rubbing his chin thoughtfully.

'Don't you think we ought to get a doctor?' asked Daphne, troubled.

He shook his head.

'She's all right, I tell you; she's sleeping – those attacks are often followed by a condition of complete exhaustion. Who is she, did you say? . . . Ella Creed . . . the name is familiar: I must have seen it on the billboards.'

He looked down at the sleeping Ella and shook his head.

'She was very attractive once,' he said. 'She must have been.'

'I think she's rather pretty now,' said Daphne.

He gave her the ghost of a smile.

'I am not an authority, I'm afraid.'

At that moment the eyelids of the sleeping girl fluttered and opened. She looked from one to the other in a dazed way, and when she spoke her voice was thick and stupid.

'What has happened?' she asked, and sat up with an effort.

'You've had a fainting attack. Would you like me to take you home?' asked Daphne.

The woman shook her head.

'No; I can go home. Will you get my car?'

She came unsteadily to her feet, the girl supporting her, Mr. Beale watching the recovery with the detachment of a scientist whose interest was quite impersonal.

'You sent your car away. Will you take a taxicab?' asked Daphne.

'No! I don't . . . don't . . .'

Ella's voice shrank from a loud protest to a mutter of sound, and she sat down heavily on the settee.

'Get a taxi,' signalled Beale, and Daphne ran out into the street.

There was no taxi in sight, but presently she espied one crawling away from her on the other side of the street, and ran towards it. She secured the machine and drove back, to find Mr. Beale standing on the doorstep.

'I think we had better let her rest for a little while. I have telephoned for a doctor, but I'm sure there is nothing to be concerned about,' he said.

After Daphne had paid off the taxi-man he followed her into the drawing-room.

'Just tell me what happened, and why did she come?'

The answer involved a certain amount of invention on Daphne's part, and she hated herself for deceiving him.

'I was going to supper with her the other night and I left the theatre early, and – and – didn't go to supper.'

'She came round to find the reason, eh?' said Mr. Beale. 'An actress . . . humph!'

He paced up and down the room, his hands behind him.

'Odd that she should be handling the Feathered Serpent when she collapsed as she did.'

He had said this before, she remembered. She did not understand why he thought the incident so 'odd.'

'Do you think she saw something in the figure?' asked Daphne. 'Something we haven't seen?'

Gregory Beale shook his head.

'Women are highly imaginative, but most of them can only imagine unpleasant things. Has that ever struck you?'

It was growing dark and she drew the curtains, and made an effort to finish the task she had set herself for the day. Once she thought she heard Ella's voice, and went to the door, but at that moment Mr. Beale's own study door closed. She wondered whether Ella was talking in her sleep. Nearly a quarter of an hour passed, and then Gregory Beale came in, a smile on his mobile mouth.

'Your young lady has made a rather rapid recovery,' he said. 'She's going home. I asked her if she'd like you to go with her, but she declined. Perhaps if you'd call a cab – she seems to have sent her own car away.'

Daphne went into the street and beckoned a passing cabman. As she did so, she was conscious that somebody standing a few yards away from the house, leaning against a lamp-post, was watching her, and she turned to see the cadaverous-looking man who had rung the bell just before Ella Creed had fainted. The man, seeing himself observed, turned his head quickly, as though to avoid recognition. He might have saved himself the trouble, for Daphne had not seen him before in her life.

When she re-entered the house, Ella was in the hall, slowly pulling on her gloves. Under the make-up the girl could see that her face was deathly white; her lower lip trembled and she almost failed to control her voice.

'Well, I'll be getting along. I'm very much obliged to you, Mr.—What's your name?'

Her hard eyes fell upon the girl, and there was something in them so unexpectedly malignant that Daphne almost gasped.

'Is that my cab?' And, when the girl replied: 'I'll be seeing you again some time,' said Ella, and with a nod passed out of the house and down the steps.

Mr. Beale watched until the cab was out of sight, and then:

'Good gracious!' he said, in mild surprise. 'That fellow hasn't gone yet!'

He indicated the hollow-cheeked stranger who was standing by the lamp-post.

'Queer,' he said, as he closed the door and followed her into the drawing-room. 'But the world is full of queer people – your Miss Ella Creed, for example – a curious woman. Do you know anybody named Lane?'

Daphne shook her head.

'She was talking about him all the time – William Lane. It has a familiar ring to me, that name. Apparently he was a convict.' He shook his head again. 'Prison is a terrible place – a great laboratory where the good are transmuted into the bad, where all the sweetest and noblest of human qualities turn sour and ugly, where kindly and simple souls become ravaging beasts.' He stopped himself. 'Dear me, I am moralising!'

He looked at his watch.

'It's time you went home, young lady. Oh, by the way, I am expecting a visit from another friend of yours to-night – Mr. Leicester Crewe. What sort of man is he?'

Daphne gave a guarded and, on the whole, charitable report.

'He wishes me to buy some South American shares – says he is anxious to leave the country in a hurry and can't wait for the ordinary market transaction. They are perfectly sound shares, but just now there is no market for them. Is he an honest man, would you say?'

She hesitated to give this character to Mr. Leicester Crewe.

'As honest as most business men,' she said, and he laughed softly at her caution.

Daphne left the house with an uncomfortable and apprehensive feeling, and, try as she did, she could not reduce her emotion to any tangible cause. Perhaps it was the thought of Ella and her mysterious illness that worried her. She stopped at a tube station, and, going into a telephone booth, found Ella's address. A bus took her to St. John's Wood, and she rang the bell of the outer gate and was admitted.

'Yes, miss,' said the maid, 'Miss Creed came home about half an hour ago. Do you want to see her?'

'No, no,' said Daphne hastily. 'I only wanted to be sure that she's all right.'

'There's nothing much the matter with her, miss,' said the maid. (It was a peculiarity of Ella Creed that she was universally detested by her servants.)

She was turning to go when a voice hailed her from the balcony. It was Ella, and, looking back, Daphne saw the woman silhouetted against the dim light in the passage.

'Olroyd!' she called. She had a disagreeable habit of calling women by their surnames. 'What do you want?'

'Nothing,' said Daphne. 'I called to see if you'd got home all right.'

'Why shouldn't I get home all right?' asked Ella querulously.

Very wisely, Daphne offered no reply, and made her escape. To her surprise, the maid followed her through the garden door, and, holding it close behind her, she lowered her voice.

'She's been having a row with somebody on the telephone – sent us all down to the kitchen so that we couldn't hear. Do you know what the trouble is, miss?'

'No,' said Daphne, a little stiffly, for she rather resented the woman's confidence.

'Her dresser's here, packing her things: she phoned for her the moment she got home. Do you know whether Miss Creed is going away?'

'I haven't the slightest idea,' said Daphne, and, turning abruptly away, ended the conversation.

Ella's house was in a very quiet thoroughfare leading from Avenue Road. There were very few pedestrians in the street, and only one car that was drawn up about twenty yards from the house. She walked quickly towards the main thoroughfare, anxious to get back to her hotel. She glanced idly at the car as she passed, and there was something about it which seemed oddly familiar.

And then in a flash she remembered: across the glass of the near side lamp was an irregular crack, like one of those pictures of a flash of lightning which unimaginative artists draw – and in that instant there came back to her a mind picture which she had not consciously registered. She had seen exactly that 'flash of lightning' crack on the near side lamp of the car which had taken her to Epping Forest. For a second she was panic-stricken . . . she wanted to run; did not even dare look at the driver as she hurried past. Faster and faster she walked, glancing apprehensively over her shoulder, but nobody followed her, and she came to the main road hot and breathless, her legs trembling under her.

She had to wait some time for her bus, and was debating whether it would be better if she walked to the Underground station, when:

'Excuse me, miss.'

She nearly jumped at the sound, and turned to find herself looking into the eyes of the hollow-faced man she had seen outside Mr. Beale's house, and whose arrival had coincided with Ella's heart attack. In that moment of panic she almost swooned, though there was nothing to be afraid of, she told herself. The street was crowded with homeward bound pedestrians – there was even a policeman in sight.

'What – what do you want?' she stammered.

'You're Mr. Beale's secretary, ain't you, miss? I've followed you from his house, and I've been trying to get a word with you.'

A terrible fit of coughing interrupted his speech. The paroxysm was such that he had to hold on to the wall for support.

'Don't worry, miss,' he wheezed at last. 'I've got a lung – if I'd had any brains I'd have stayed out in the Argentine, where you do get a bit of sunshine! I wouldn't have come at all, only my sister persuaded me, and now I'm trying to raise the money to get back.'

'Didn't you come to Mr. Beale's house this afternoon?' she asked.

'That's right, miss,' he nodded. 'Lord, ain't he changed! The last time I spoke to him he'd have took off his coat and given it to a poor fellow, but to-day he sort of snapped me up!'

He was not at all formidable at close quarters: he looked what he was, a poor wreck of a consumptive, who shivered under his thin coat at every errant gust of wind.

Her bus had come and passed. Daphne felt a sudden curiosity concerning this creature; perhaps it was kindled by his strange interpretation of Gregory Beale's character.

'Mr. Beale is very kind. You must have said something that annoyed him,' she said.

'I don't know.' The man was so dispirited, so wretchedly ill that he could hardly work up interest in his remarks. 'He's not usually like that. If you could say a word for me, miss, perhaps he'd help me. I told him where I was living.'

'What is your name?' she asked.

'Harry Merstham, miss – commonly called in the old days Harry the Barman. I was bar-tender in Buenos Ayres. A gentleman got me the job – Mr. Billy Lewston – ever heard of him?'

She shook her head.

'He was a hook, and so was his sister,' said Harry the Barman calmly, and she gathered that Mr. Lewston had belonged to the light-fingered brotherhood.

'I got this job in Buenos Ayres to-day and I left England, as you might say, to-morrow. I've been very ill there, and I thought Mr. Beale knew—'

Again a fit of coughing arrested his speech. When he recovered, he was, he told her, penniless, and in a moment of pity she gave him five shillings, took his address, and promised to speak to Mr. Beale in the morning; a promise she repented later, for she had no right, she told herself, to plead for a man whom her employer probably knew much better than she.

Her first act on reaching the hotel was to telephone to Peter, but Peter was neither at his lodgings nor at the office. Undeterred, she put a call through to his club, only to learn that she had missed him by five minutes.

She wanted to tell him of Ella Creed, for she felt that she was not being disloyal to Mr. Beale in relating what had happened, and which might have an important bearing upon Peter's investigation into the mystery of the Feathered Serpent. Had she managed to reach him, it is possible she would have told him, as an item of gossip, her encounter with the cadaverous Harry Merstham, but when she was in her room and thinking matters over, she decided that this would have been mischievous gossip, reflecting as it did upon the generosity of her employer. And yet, had she realised it, the appearance of Harry the Barman was the most important development in the case, and a few minutes' talk with him might have supplied the missing links of the chain which Peter Dewin was vainly endeavouring to join.

When she came down for dinner she remembered to call at the little bureau for letters, and had to wait a minute or two whilst an American lady sought information of the manager, who happened to be in the office. There were many tourist families at the hotel, some of them, if not wealthy, at least very well to do, and the American, a pretty woman of forty, the type which America alone seems able to produce, was discussing jewellery.

'. . . I'll put them into the hotel safe with pleasure, madam,' the manager was saying, 'but I always advise guests who are staying in London for any time to hire a box at the Safe Deposit if the jewellery is very valuable, as yours is.'

The lady was interested and asked questions.

'It is very simple,' said the manager, and explained the procedure. Daphne listened, and, listening, the light of understanding dawned upon her, and turning abruptly, she almost ran to the telephone booth and made a fourth and unsuccessful attempt to get into touch with Peter.

XIX

Friendship with high officers of Scotland Yard is something of a liability, as Peter Dewin realised as he sat meekly in Superintendent Clarke's office and listened to a lecture delivered by that stern man.

'Nobody knows better than you, Peter, that you ought to communicate every single item to me. I've put you on to some of the best stories you've ever written—'

'Did I phone for you to interview the Lightfoot gentleman?' asked Peter gently. 'Haven't I given you a new line?'

'You've given me red herrings,' growled Clarke. And then, in a more conciliatory tone: 'Now, Peter, what do you know that you haven't told me?'

'There are so many things that you don't know,' said Peter insultingly, 'that I hardly know where to begin. For instance, there is the concrete house in Epping Forest, and there's the gold ring with the wheatsheaves, and Mr. Bone, who's dead – I've discovered he was a public-house loafer who lurched from one saloon in Tidal Basin to another until death cut short his activities – and the more mysterious Harry the Barman, employed by Joe Farmer, who made a sudden and sensational disappearance from England two days before the arrest of William Lane. There is William Lane himself, killed at Thatcham and resurrected at Grosvenor Square; a perfect type of the perfect criminal – a man who foresees all contingencies and prepares for them—'

'You've told me about William Lane,' interrupted Clarke, 'and I've had him traced. He was killed in a motor accident a few days after his release from Dartmoor—'

Peter shook his head.

'He was not killed. There were three men who stuck together closer than brothers; there was Harry the Lag – who is not to be confused with Harry the Barman – William Lane, and the man Hugg. Harry the Lag thought that Lane would be a gold-mine to him, and probably he was right. My own feeling is that when Lane was released he could not shake off his companions in durance, and that he sought a dozen ways of disappearing before a badly driven motor-car supplied the means of escape. William Lane is alive and in London. He has already killed the man who was the principal witness against him.'

Clarke nodded his agreement.

'I'll be candid with you, Dewin – I accept that theory of yours. Now what's this stuff about Harry the Barman?'

Peter offered a few explanations which were not particularly illuminating. Mr. Clarke said as much, and Peter agreed.

'They don't even illuminate me, most of 'em,' he said ruefully; 'but I feel they're all strings that lead to the main piece.'

When he got to the office he learnt that Daphne had telephoned to him, and he was at the instrument, getting her number, when a call came through. It was not from Daphne: he recognised the voice immediately.

'Is that Mr. Dewin? . . . I'm Gregory Beale. I wonder if you could come to my house at nine o'clock to-night? I have been rather worried, though it seems absurd, by the receipt of one of those stupid cards.'

For the moment Peter was staggered.

'Not a Feathered Serpent card?' he asked.

'Yes; and it is curiously inscribed. In fact, I have asked Superintendent Clarke, who I understand is in charge of this Farmer murder, to come along at the same time.'

Peter hung up the receiver, frowning thoughtfully, and for a moment Daphne Olroyd went out of his mind.

He went back to his typewriter, but the story he had planned to write came haltingly – he read the first page and found it so un-utterably dull that he rubbed it into a ball, threw it into the waste-paper basket and started again. His second attempt was only a little more successful. He carried the second failure to the night editor, and was very frank about its demerits.

'Probably I'll have a better story to tell after I've seen Beale,' he said. 'For the moment I have stopped being brilliant.'

As he mounted the steps of the Beale house he saw a short, thick-set man ringing the bell. He was a stranger to Peter, and when Mr. Beale opened the door to admit them he was not greatly surprised to learn the visitor's profession.

'I'd like you to meet Mr. Holden, my lawyer,' said Beale.

He ushered them into the drawing-room, which had been Daphne's workshop during the day.

'It would be better if we waited until Mr. Clarke arrives,' he began, when a ring of the bell sent him hurrying to the door to admit the genial superintendent.

The first impression that Peter received was that Mr. Gregory Beale was strangely nervous. This he betrayed in his voice and in every gesture.

'I suppose you'll think that I am making a fuss about nothing,' he said, as he took from his pocket a card of familiar shape. 'This kind of thing you have seen before, Superintendent, but I would like you to read what is typewritten on the back.'

Clarke took the card, fixed his pince-nez, and Peter, without asking permission, read the card over the superintendent's shoulder. It ran:

> *Leicester Crewe, whose real name is Lewston, is calling on you at half-past nine to sell you shares in a Buenos Ayres Tramway Corporation. You are incurring a double risk in receiving him: the risk of injury to yourself and death to him.*

'I found it in the passage; it had been pushed under the door. It must have been about seven or eight o'clock to-night,' said Beale. 'My first impulse was to treat it with contempt and throw it into the fire. It then occurred to me as remarkable that anybody but

Mr. Crewe and I should know that he was calling, and the nature of his business. Naturally, my secretary, who is not unknown to you' – he smiled at Peter – 'was aware that I expected him, but I can think of nobody else.'

'One of his own clerks,' suggested Clarke, and Mr. Beale nodded.

'That, of course, is possible. I am a little nervous about it, and for this reason I have asked you to come, and particularly my solicitor, Mr. Holden. If there is to be any transfer of shares I should like the document inspected.'

The lawyer laughed.

'You're getting cautious as the years go on, Mr. Beale,' he said, with a twinkle in his eyes, and his client seemed secretly amused.

'I have in the past been rather a reckless person, but that is one of the disadvantages of having too much money.' And then, in a more serious tone: 'My suggestion is that you gentlemen should remain here whilst I interview Mr. Crewe. I shall leave my study door ajar, and if I see anything that causes me the least suspicion, I will call for you. It is very childish of me, but this wretched serpent is also getting on my nerves.'

He excused himself and went into his study to collect some papers which he wished the lawyer to see.

'I've never known Beale like that.' The lawyer shook his head. 'Nothing ever scared him – and as to recklessness! The pet hobby of his younger days was to build model dwellings for the poor—'

Peter with difficulty suppressed an exclamation.

'—He wouldn't consult his lawyer or even his banker. In fact, he got so resentful at a suggestion his bank manager made that he changed his bank. He built Lion House, and nobody knew who was the philanthropist who had spent sixty thousand pounds to provide young girls of the East End with lodgings, except myself – not even his bank manager was aware of his munificence.'

'He had a friend who was an architect?' ventured Peter.

The lawyer nodded.

'Yes, Mr. Walber, another eccentric gentleman – perhaps I

oughtn't to describe Mr. Beale as eccentric, but in the days when he was an enthusiastic slummer, he spent money like water. If he hadn't gone back to South American researches he would have ruined himself!'

Beale came back just then and put an end to the personal gossip, so interesting to Peter. The transfers that he had prepared were in order except that blanks were left for the number of shares to be transferred, nor was the amount to be paid inscribed on the receipt.

'They seem to be in order,' said Mr. Holden, looking over his glasses.

At that moment there was a rat-tat at the outer door, and for some unaccountable reason Peter Dewin's flesh crept and a cold shiver went down his spine. He was amazed at himself, and could not recall any parallel to this experience.

Beale hurried from the room, and presently they heard Leicester Crewe's voice. He was talking in his politest tone.

'. . . I'm very sorry to bother you at such a late hour, Mr. Beale, but I have to go out of England rather suddenly, and I may be away for some months . . .'

The voices faded as Beale led the way into the study.

'That's Crewe all right—' began Clarke under his breath. 'He is – good God!'

From the direction of the study came a shrill scream of agony that ended in a choking sob. The sound of a thud, and Beale's voice calling for help. In an instant Clarke had leapt from the room, followed by Peter, and, flying along the passage, ran in at the study door.

Beale was standing by the fire-place, looking with a set face at the figure of Leicester Crewe, huddled in a heap against the wall opposite the French windows.

'What happened?' asked Clarke as he bent over the prostrate man.

'I don't know . . . he gave a scream and fell. I saw and heard nothing. . . . It happened the moment we entered the study.'

'Switch on all the lights,' said Clarke, and Peter obeyed.

The superintendent laid the prostrate figure flat and made a brief examination.

'He's been shot.' He lifted his hand, wet with blood. 'Through the heart!'

'Dead?' It was the lawyer's hollow voice.

Clarke nodded.

'I think so. Phone for a doctor, somebody.'

Peter knew a doctor in the neighbourhood and got through to him without delay. When he returned, Clarke was by the window, examining the glass. He pointed to a neat round hole in the middle of a star-like crack.

'Shot through the window,' he said. 'This is unsplinterable glass, isn't it?'

Beale nodded.

'Yes. I had it put in after some boys threw stones over the wall and nearly hit my face.'

He looked back at the thing that lay on the floor.

'Dead!' he said slowly.

'Did you hear an explosion?' asked Clarke, and when Beale shook his head Clarke unfastened the French windows carefully, stepped down into the garden, and Peter, who never went abroad in the winter without a pocket-lamp, provided the means of illumination.

A stretch of crazy pavement led to the wall at the back; there was no sign of the murderer, and the only place where a person might take refuge was a very small brick shed, which was padlocked on the outside.

On a side path leading to the main crazy pavement Clarke saw something glitter in the light of his lamp, and, stooping, picked it up. It was the exploded shell of an automatic pistol. Taking a pencil from his pocket, he made a big cross exactly on the spot where the shell was discovered.

'That's that,' he said with satisfaction. 'We shall have to wait till daylight before we can examine the walls properly. Peter, you'd better phone to the local station and get a couple of men here; and I'm afraid, my boy, you'll have to make yourself scarce.'

'If I make myself scarce,' said Peter quietly, 'you'll never catch the man who killed Leicester Crewe.'

There was a silence.

'You're serious?' questioned Clarke. He had an immense respect for the reporter, and he had never known Peter to make so definite a statement without justification.

'I am the most serious man you have met to-night,' said Peter. 'I don't know how the regulations stand about my being around, but I think you'd be wise to stretch a point. I shall have to go away, naturally, because I've got to pick up a few threads elsewhere, but I want permission to come back when you begin your search in the morning. You won't regret it.'

The superintendent hesitated. He had not yet grown accustomed to his own supremacy, nor was he fully conscious of the fact that he had the right now, without consulting a superior, to adopt a line of action which, before his promotion, he would have hesitated to sanction.

'All right,' he said; 'phone the Yard and the local station.'

Peter went back through the study. Leicester Crewe lay motionless, and it only needed a glance at his white face to see that Clarke's hurried diagnosis was correct – Leicester Crewe had passed beyond the reach of human justice.

Peter was using the hall telephone when the two men-servants, who had been out all day, returned, to find Mr. Beale in the drawing-room with his lawyer, and he had recovered something of his calmness.

'I don't wish to discuss the matter,' he said. 'It will be in the newspapers, of course – I don't seem to be able to keep out of the newspapers!'

'There was no discussion, was there, between Mr. Crewe and yourself, Mr. Beale?'

Beale shook his head.

'No; as a matter of fact, he was still thanking me for receiving him when he fell. I have no very clear idea of what happened,' he admitted frankly.

'You heard no report, no shot?'

'None.' Beale was emphatic. 'If I had heard it, you must have heard it too,' he said, which was true. There had been not the slightest hint of an explosion; that soul-racking shriek and Beale's call for help had been the first intimation that they, in the drawing-room, had had of the tragedy.

Peter hurried from the house, and, chartering a cab, drove to Daphne Olroyd's hotel. She had gone to bed, he learnt, but his urgent note brought her down in ten minutes fully dressed. Fortunately, at this hour the lounge was deserted and they had a secluded corner to themselves, and in a few words Peter told the horrified girl of what had happened at Beale's house that night.

'I hate making use of you, my dear, but I want you to rack your brains and tell me of any little incident you have witnessed that you may have overlooked; any unusual caller who has come to the house; any workmen who may have been employed in the garden . . .'

Daphne thought hard. The only thing she could recall about the garden was Mr. Beale's habit of walking in the morning and picking off dead leaves.

'He used to make a little fire of them every other day – all this is stupidly trivial,' she began, but he was emphatic in denying this.

'Nothing is too trivial. Did Leicester Crewe ever come to the house before?'

'Never.'

'None of that crowd – Ella Creed—'

'Why, yes,' she said. 'I meant to tell you; I called you up, but you were out.'

'Yes, yes; what happened to Ella Creed?' he asked, in a fever of impatience.

He listened without interruption until she had finished.

'She had a Feathered Serpent in her hand, did she?' he asked slowly. 'And was looking at it – what an odd coincidence!'

She opened her eyes wide at this.

'How curious you should say that! Mr. Beale used the same words exactly. There was a man at the door to whom Mr. Beale was speaking.'

'Could you describe him?'

She nodded triumphantly.

'That's the second thing I had to tell you. I know him, and know his name. He followed me to Ella Creed's house – apparently he knew Mr. Beale in the old days and wanted him to help him return to the Argentine.'

Peter was staring at her.

'And all this happened when Mr. Beale and the caller were talking on the doorstep,' he said slowly. 'Ella Creed had the Feathered Serpent in her hand – and fainted! That's the oddest coincidence you'll ever meet with. You know the name of this ghastly looking stranger? I don't suppose he was anybody important.' He knit his brows. 'But he came from the Argentine . . .'

'His name was Mr. Merstham,' she said.

Peter shook his head.

'It means nothing to me.'

'Harry Merstham. His other name is Harry the Barman—'

'What?'

He half rose from his chair in his excitement and glared down at her until she was alarmed.

'Is he – anybody?' she faltered.

'Harry the Barman! Where does he live?'

She had written down the address; it was in her bag upstairs, and, leaving him for a moment, she returned with the information.

'Is he very important?' she asked.

Peter nodded; his face was lit, transfigured; those lazy eyes of his were sparklingly alive.

'There's nothing else you can tell me? Heaven knows you've told me enough!' he said as he slipped the card into his pocket. 'Nothing extraordinary . . . fantastical . . . nothing?'

Then she remembered one insignificant incident.

'The door is hardly worth mentioning—' she began.

'Everything is worth mentioning,' he interrupted. 'What door?'

'It is a little door that used to be in the garden wall. Mr. Beale was painting it with Aztec designs. They were rather hideous,' she smiled, 'but he got an extraordinary pleasure in painting them.'

'Where did he have the door – in the garden? Or in the study? The place had a painty smell.'

'In the study,' she replied. 'It made the room reek of paint, and it was rather disagreeable for a little while.'

His mind was working at lightning speed.

'Where did he put the door when it was painted?' And she told him.

'When did you see it last in the study?'

She thought for a moment.

'This afternoon,' she said. 'Mr. Beale said he was moving it to the shed. The smell was rather disagreeable and seemed to permeate the whole house.'

Peter took a sheet of paper from his pocket and drew a rough plan of the room.

'Just show me where the door was when he was working on it.'

She indicated the spot and he marked this, folded the paper and smiled delightedly.

'There's one more thing.' She put her hand on his arm as he was rising, and he found himself patting her hand gently. 'The car with the zigzag crack – the lamp, I mean. I saw that very near Ella's house to-night. I'm positive it was the same machine.'

'One minute,' said Peter.

In another second he was telephoning to the Orpheum stage door. It was too late for the box office, and the stage door would supply all the news he wanted.

'No, sir,' said the stage-door porter in reply to his question, 'Miss Creed did not appear to-night. She's been taken ill and had to go away into the country.'

'Did she come to the theatre at all?' asked Peter.

'No, she phoned.'

Without a second's delay he rang up Ella's house, and her maid answered him.

'I can't understand it, sir. They called up from the theatre to ask how Miss Creed was. So far as I know, she's all right – a little upset this afternoon by something or other, but otherwise all right.'

'Did she leave for the theatre at the usual time?' asked Peter.

'Yes, sir.'

He hung up with a grim smile. The Feathered Serpent had been a busy man that night.

XX

He did not tell the girl about Ella, but left her almost immediately afterwards.

'What time do you breakfast?' he asked, and when she told him nine, he promised to come. 'I shall be up all night on this case, and maybe I shall think of something I want to ask you.'

He was gone before she realised that the one piece of information she wished to give to him had entirely slipped from her memory.

By the time he got back to the house he found it practically in police occupation, and he had some difficulty in getting a note through to Clarke. Eventually he was admitted. Mr. Beale had gone up to his room, rather overcome, the staid butler told him, by the events of the evening. The body had been removed, he was relieved to find, as he passed through the study and joined the little party of searchers in the garden.

Somebody had procured two powerful garage lamps, and with these the police were making a systematic search. When Peter joined the superintendent, he and Sweeney were examining marks on the brickwork.

'That's where he came over,' said Sweeney. 'Look at those sacks.'

He pointed upwards; three thick sacks had been laid over the broken glass at the top of the wall, and when these were removed it was seen that the glass itself had been carefully chipped off – they found fragments both inside and outside the garden.

'Brilliant!' said Peter admiringly, and Sweeney, for the first time conscious of his presence, turned with a snort.

'I don't see anything brilliant in that. The sacks were laid to make the getaway easy. I should imagine a rope was thrown over and held by somebody on the other side.'

'What is your theory, Mr. Clarke?' asked Peter.

'The same as Sweeney's,' said the superintendent. 'I'll probably change it in the morning, but for the moment the story I shall give to the Press is that somebody got over the wall and was concealed in the garden, and waited till Crewe came into the room. There are no blinds to the study, the room is well lit, and every movement in the room would be visible to a man in hiding. Mr. Crewe entered the room first—'

'There was no light in the passage,' said Peter promptly.

'What's that to do with it?' asked Sweeney. 'Anyway, he couldn't have been seen in the passage, and certainly couldn't have been shot in the passage.'

'I'm only pointing out that there was no light in the passage, and there was a lot of light in the study. When you told me to switch them on, there was only one set that weren't lit – the wall brackets – which made very little difference to the general illumination.'

'There was sufficient light in the study, at any rate, for the murderer to have seen Crewe when he entered the room,' said Clarke patiently. 'The darkness of the passage means nothing, does it?'

Peter did not reply.

There followed a quarter of an hour of measurement and note-taking, and then the reporter asked if they had the key of the little shed.

'We've opened that and had a good look round,' said Sweeney. 'There's nothing there but a few garden tools and an old door.'

'That's what I want to see – the old door.'

The shed was unlocked and he stooped his way in, for the entrance was low. Leaning against the brick end of the shed he saw the door glistening with new paint, a terrifying object if he had not been prepared for the hideous daub of a face that had been painted in the centre. Radiating from this were a number of irregular designs made up of birds and flowers – he thought it was not unlike some of the old Egyptian drawings he had seen in the Luxor tombs. The paint was still wet when, using a penknife to help him, he began to probe the door with the blade. He had the shed to himself for five minutes, and then Sweeney joined him.

'What the devil are you trying to do?' asked the stout police officer.

'Nothing very much,' said Peter, putting his penknife back into his pocket. 'These primitive paintings rather interest me.'

'Primitive paintings!' growled the other. 'Isn't a murder good enough for you, or are you doing an art story?'

Peter did not reply; he came out, fixed the hasp that fastened the door, turned the key in the padlock and handed it back to Sweeney.

He was in his office till one o'clock in the morning, and for an hour and a half his typewriter rattled incessantly, and this time he had written a story of which any star reporter might be proud.

'The trouble with me,' he said to the night man who 'subbed' the last page of his copy, 'is that I can't be in two places at once. This is the third time in my brilliant career that I wish I had been born twins.'

The cab he had chartered earlier in the evening, and which had already accumulated an immense liability, took him to the address which Daphne had given to him – the temporary home of Harry the Barman. It was in a little street in Poplar, and it was a long time before his knocking brought a stout and scantily attired lady to the door.

'I want to speak to Mr. Merstham,' said Peter, after preliminary apologies.

'He's gone,' was the startling reply. 'A messenger come for him about nine o'clock, and he packed his bag and went.'

'Did he pay his bill?' asked Peter quickly.

The landlady was not as surprised as one more favourably placed might have been at this question, nor did she seem to regard it as impertinent.

'He did, and more,' she said with satisfaction.

'In other words, he gave you—?' Peter waited expectantly.

'That's my business,' snapped the woman. And then, in a changed tone: 'I suppose he come by it honest; he gave me a five-pound note, mister. You're not the police?'

'No, I'm not the police, but I should be very much obliged to you if you could tell me the number of the note.'

She went inside, shutting the door in his face, but meant no discourtesy, for poor people have a rooted antipathy to leaving their doors open in the middle of the night. When she came back, it was to give him the selvedge of a newspaper on which she had scrawled a number of figures.

'Thank you,' said Peter.

'He didn't pinch it, did he, mister? He owed me three weeks' rent, anyway.'

Peter reassured her as best he could.

'He didn't leave anything behind him – any letter or paper of any kind?'

'Only the envelope that the letter came in. I saw that,' said the woman after a minute's thought. 'Would you like to see it, mister?'

Again the door was closed, and, after keeping him for an unconscionable time, the woman returned and handed him a crumpled envelope.

'If this money ain't come by honest—' she began.

'I'm perfectly sure he got it honestly; you needn't worry about that.'

He told the cabman to stop at the first coffee stall in Commercial Road, and, getting down, he asked the driver to order refreshment for both, whilst he examined the envelope. It was addressed to 'H. Merstham, 99, Little Hitchfold Street, Poplar.' The address was typewritten; the envelope bore the stamp of a messenger company; but what interested Peter was that it had retained something of the shape it had been when it was received. It must have been a very fat letter, he concluded, and would have been surprised if it had not been.

'Gucumatz?' – 'Gucumatz' and the key. Those were the two blank places in the story, and since they were vital to continuity, this biggest mystery of all must be cleared up before the story was clear and denial-proof.

It was daylight at seven o'clock, and he spent the intervening time sketching out the big story that was to be told, he hoped, on the morrow. In the raw morning he knocked at the door of Beale's house and was admitted by a detective who knew him.

'Mr. Clarke and Mr. Sweeney have gone home,' he was informed. 'They told me, if you came, that you weren't to touch anything.'

'Is Mr. Beale awake yet?'

'He's in his study, having his coffee,' said the police officer, and Peter, knocking at the study door, was invited to come in.

Evidently the murder of Leicester Crewe had succeeded in disturbing the philosophic calm of the scientist. He looked as if he had not slept, and his first words were a confession of this failure.

'I am glad you came,' he said. 'I wanted to get your view on this crime – and the criminal. It has since occurred to me that possibly the shot was not intended for Crewe at all.'

'But for you?' suggested Peter, and shook his head smilingly. 'No, I don't think we need entertain that theory for a minute,' he said. 'I suppose, Mr. Beale, you're regretting that you left Central America?'

Gregory Beale was stirring his coffee slowly, and now he raised his eyes.

'I was asking myself that very question in the middle of the night, and I decided to answer it in the negative! To pass a sheltered life, free from such tragedies as we witnessed last night, is not the best way of spending existence. They are painful experiences, but vitally necessary to get life into perspective. They also have another value which I will not discuss, in case you are shocked.'

Peter was not in the mood for philosophy at that hour of the morning.

'Mr. Beale, do you know a man named Harry Merstham – Harry the Barman?'

Beale nodded at once.

'Yes, he was on my conscience last night, and still a little on my conscience this morning. He came to me yesterday for help to get back to South America, and I'm afraid I was rather brusque with him. I repented last night and sent him a little money – in fact, I sent him a hundred pounds,' he smiled. 'That doesn't entirely relieve me of reproach. I hurt him and rather shocked him by my rudeness, and impressions are ineradicable.'

'Did you know him very well?'

Beale shook his head.

'Not very well. He is rather a thriftless fellow, who drifted from one bar to another. He was a bar-tender of sorts. But I was sorry for him; he has a weak chest, and wanted me to send him to South Africa. I suppose he wasn't sufficiently amusing. A philanthropist is not wholly disinterested. He likes to have the glow of helping interesting people. It is so much more satisfactory to give up your seat in a car to a young and pretty girl than to offer the same courtesy to a grimy old charwoman!'

Peter laughed at this.

'He drifted out of my sight, and I'd forgotten all about him. I suppose I have lost the philanthropic mood; so that when he made his appearance yesterday I was rather' – he paused to find a word – 'outraged. It was like the ghost of a dead folly arising to mock one. "Folly" is a rather violent word to use in that connection,' he corrected himself, 'only – I have lost touch with the poor, their troubles, their needs and their sorrows. It is lamentable, but a fact.'

'Where is Merstham to be found?' asked Peter.

Mr. Beale shook his head.

'I don't know. I could give you his address; I have it on my desk somewhere.' He searched among some papers. 'Here it is.' He handed Peter a half-sheet of paper on which he had scribbled three lines of writing. But the reporter did not look at the paper.

'I know the address. I went to see him in the early hours of the morning – he left his lodgings last night.'

The philanthropist seemed amused at this.

'And a very wise man, if my memory of Poplar is right. He talked of going to South Africa. At least, that was the impression I gained during the short conversation I had with him.'

Peter drew up a chair uninvited, and seated himself on the other side of the desk opposite the philosopher.

'You talked about shocking me just now – I wonder if you'll be shocked if I tell you that, given a knowledge of Farmer's and Crewe's offences, I could take a very sympathetic view of those two murders?'

Beale's eyebrows rose.

'I'm surprised to hear you say that. I thought you were on the side of law and order.'

His eyes were twinkling; the sensitive lips twitched as though with an effort he was suppressing a smile.

'I thought so last night,' Peter went on, 'when I was looking around your garden with the police; when, in fact, I was inspecting your door painting.'

Mr. Beale's face was blank.

'My door painting? What on earth—?' And then, with a laugh: 'Oh, I see what you mean. Miss Olroyd has been telling you about my little hobby. She's a very nice girl. Are you – er—'

Peter did not help him.

'Are you very serious about Miss Olroyd?'

'Terribly serious,' said Peter earnestly, and the older man nodded.

He had a very grave and rather sweet expression at times. Peter used to wonder, when he first met him, whether he had been crossed in love in his early youth, and had dismissed that romantic possibility as a piece of deplorable mushiness.

'You look tired, Mr. Dewin.' His voice was sympathetic. 'I wish you would go home and have a long sleep.'

The last sentence was very deliberately spoken, and Peter understood.

Nevertheless, he was waiting for Daphne when she came down, and they breakfasted together in the long, low-roofed dining-room of the hotel. The girl was a little worried. She had had a message from Mr. Beale that she was not to go that day nor the next – 'until,' his note ran, 'the smell of tragedy has been blown out of the house.'

'You haven't been to bed,' she accused him. 'Have you got your story?'

'Not quite,' he said, as he unfolded his serviette. And then, to his amazement, she leaned over towards him. 'I know the secret of Gucumatz.'

'You know the secret of Gucumatz?' he repeated. 'Then you've run to earth the only mystery that I can't bring into line with my many deductions.'

'I know what "Gucumatz" means, I know what the key means,' she said; 'but I'm not going to tell you till you've finished your breakfast, or you'll be dashing away and leaving me.'

He did not take her seriously, and dawdled through the breakfast. She was a very pleasant companion: he realised that more and more every time he saw her, and dared tell of his conversation with Beale that morning.

'He asked me if I was serious about you. It was rather nice of him to take that interest, don't you think?'

She deftly changed the conversation.

'And now for your secret,' he said, as he began sipping his second cup of coffee.

' "Gucumatz" is a password,' she said, and he put down his cup.

'To where?' he asked.

'To a Safe Deposit.'

Peter's mouth opened wide.

'Good Lord!' he gasped. 'I never thought of that. Not that I know anything about safe deposits – but the key!' He smote the table and set the cutlery dancing.

'I only heard last night by accident,' she said. 'One of the guests here was talking to the manager, and he explained to her how a safe deposit is worked. Every client receives a key to his box and also a password by which he can satisfy the janitor that he is the owner of the box. The keys, as a rule, have a number, which is quite different from the number of the box. When you want to get anything out of the safe deposit, you first of all give the password, which is checked by the janitor against your name, and you are admitted. If you don't happen to be the person who has made the deposit, you bring a note authorising you to open the box, but you still must bring the password and produce the key.'

He sat staring at her, not uttering a word.

'You marvellous girl!' he breathed. 'Of course! What a fool I was! But, honestly, I know nothing about safe deposits, and I should never have guessed that in a hundred years.'

She saw his lips moving as though he were speaking to himself, and from time to time he nodded. Then he got up.

'Do you know where I'm going?' he asked.

'If you're a wise man—' she began.

'I'm not wise,' said Peter gravely. 'I'm going to bed, and I shall be asleep until—' he looked at his watch – 'five o'clock this evening.'

XXI

He was as good as his word. By the time he reached his lodgings the house-cleaning was in full swing, and he had an interview with his landlady which resulted in the cleaning operations being suspended in his part of the premises. After he had got into his pyjamas and drawn the shades, he rang up the exchange and asked that his private line should be interrupted until five, and with his mind free, and not even a frantic news editor to disturb him, he crawled between the sheets and was asleep even as he drew the coverings over him.

It was dark when he woke at the knocking of the door. A maid wheeled in a tea trolley and brought an evening newspaper, which he scanned as he sat up in bed. The maid went out, to return with the information that Mr. Clarke had rung up twice in the course of the afternoon. Peter called the exchange and got himself reconnected, and soon afterwards was talking to Scotland Yard.

'You'll miss a good story if you don't see me,' said Clarke.

'What has happened?'

'Come along to Scotland Yard. I can't tell you on the telephone, and I don't know whether I ought to tell you at all.'

Peter dressed at his leisure and set forth, a giant refreshed, for the Thames Embankment. There was a fog on the streets – not a heavy one, but quite sufficient to indicate that somewhere in the centre of London it was thicker.

He found Superintendent Clarke alone.

'Shut the door, will you?' growled Clarke. 'I've been trying to get you all the afternoon. You don't deserve a friend at head-quarters.'

'I was asleep and out to all the world,' said Peter.

'There are one or two items that will interest you. The first and most sensational – I suppose you'll make a sensation of it – is that the bullet the doctor has extracted from Crewe was – what do you think?'

'It was made of gold,' said Peter calmly, and Superintendent Clarke fell back in his chair.

'Sweeney told you?'

Peter shook his head.

'No, I guessed it might be. Also it did not fit the shell you found in the garden.'

Clarke shook his head.

'You *have* seen Sweeney!' he accused. 'Don't try to put any of that Doctor Watson stuff over on me. I didn't know Sweeney had seen you, but it *was* gold, and it didn't fit the shell.'

'I tell you I haven't seen Sweeney. I got all that out of my inner consciousness,' said Peter. 'What is your next sensation?'

'Ella Creed has disappeared. The management are rather worried about it, though I think this may be only an advertising stunt.'

Peter smiled.

'That is not a hard one either. I knew that she had disappeared last night – I can pretty well guess where she is. The moment I can see an Ordnance map of Essex I shall be sure.'

He met Clarke's frowning eyes without flinching.

'Produce your third sensation,' he said.

'There is no third sensation,' snapped Clarke. 'Come on, out with it, Peter. What is the story?'

'I don't think I can tell you that without the permission of Mr. Gregory Beale—'

'You can't get at him,' said Clarke. 'He's gone away to the country; he went at noon to-day and I saw him off.'

'Did he go with or without his butler?' asked Peter, interested.

'The butler went with him.'

Peter nodded.

'I should have imagined he would – the butler has been in Mr. Beale's service since he was a child, and is, I imagine, the only true-blue family retainer left in England. Where has Mr. Beale gone?'

'He has a house in Devonshire,' said Clarke impatiently. 'I've got his address, if you want to get into touch with him.'

Peter shook his head.

'I don't particularly, but I should like you to accompany me to Mr. Beale's house, and I will show you a variety of that curious insect, the Feathered Serpent, which may startle but will certainly interest you.'

Sweeney came in as they were leaving, and the three men drove together to Beale's house. The conversation was entirely supplied by the detectives, Peter maintaining, for him, a remarkable silence.

'The only thing I can't understand,' said Sweeney, 'is the absence of a report. It wasn't heard outside in the street, and even a silencer makes some sort of noise.'

It was here that Peter spoke.

'He was not killed by an automatic pistol, with or without a silencer,' he said. 'Leicester Crewe was shot dead by a Deloraine.'

'What the devil's a Deloraine?' asked Clarke.

'A Deloraine,' explained Peter, 'and why it is called a Deloraine I do not know – is a type of German air pistol that was used on certain fronts during night raids. It was abandoned because it was ineffective beyond a range which the German authorities thought was too short. At half a dozen paces, however, it will put a bullet through an inch and a half of pine; it will certainly kill a man.'

'But,' protested Sweeney, 'Crewe was killed from outside the room. There's the hole in the glass—'

'A golden bullet is a soft bullet, my friend,' said Peter gently, 'and it would mushroom with any resistance. The hole in the glass was neatly punctured with a steel bullet. Not even the most unsplinterable of patent glasses would survive the impact of gold fired at short range. Now I should like to see the door.'

'Which door?' asked Clarke, who had forgotten Peter's curiosity of the night before.

'That painted thing in the shed,' said Sweeney, amused. 'What do you expect to find there, Peter?'

'The steel bullet that punctured the window,' was Peter's cool reply. 'I rather fancy it will be pretty low down in the door. The resistance of the glass would lower the trajectory . . . somewhere about a foot from the bottom, I should imagine. I hadn't an opportunity of discovering it last night.'

He led the way through the garden to the little shed, and with Sweeney holding the light he began to probe nearer the bottom of the door, and presently:

'Here it is!'

The point of his knife had struck something hard.

'A nail,' suggested Clarke.

Peter did not answer, but began carving through the new paint, and presently hooked out a shining steel projectile.

'That wouldn't fit the shell either,' said Sweeney, examining the bullet.

Peter shook his head.

'No, but you will find that it is exactly the same size as the gold bullet.'

'Now, Peter,' said Clarke, when they were back in the study, 'we'll have a few facts. Who fired the shot that killed Mr. Crewe?'

Peter drew a long breath.

'The only man who could have fired it; the only man who was near enough to kill him with an air pistol – Gregory Beale!'

There was a deep silence.

'Do you seriously suggest that Mr. Beale murdered this man?' asked Sweeney incredulously. 'That's rather a tall order, isn't it? Why should he?'

'I am not absolutely sure why he should. I'm only certain that he did. And if you're going to wire the Devonshire police to arrest and detain Gregory Beale, I think you can save yourself the trouble. Beale is not in Devonshire, he's well out of this country by now; and in a way I'm sorry. He's the only perfect criminal I've met in my lifetime.'

XXII

A hired car was waiting at the door, and after he had made an appointment to meet the two men at Scotland Yard, he took his seat by the driver, and the powerful machine went swiftly in the direction of Regent's Park. They passed through Holloway and Wood Green, and presently they struck the Epping road. There was no need yet to make inquiries. Daphne Olroyd had practically located the position of the house to which she had been taken when, looking through the blurred window, she had seen the high wireless masts – a contingency for which her captors had not allowed, or else perhaps they were so sure that she would not escape to carry her story back, that they were careless.

They passed through the silent village and the car slowed, whilst, with the aid of a swivelled spotlight, Peter searched the hedge for the opening.

'Here it is,' he said at last, and the machine turned into a narrow track.

There was a check when they reached the point where the track broke off in two directions, but Peter, getting down from the car, made an examination of the ground under the brilliant rays of the lamp. The wheel tracks leading to the right were obviously made by farm wagons; on the left were distinct marks of motor-car tyres, and to the left he went, keeping the light shining ahead. They might have passed the house, hidden as it was in a clump of trees, but Peter had kept the light fixed upon the motor-car markings, and he saw that they branched left across a patch of grass into the wood, and he followed, and was rewarded when, in the glare of the headlamps, a squat, rambling and very new one-storeyed house was revealed.

Seemingly it was built of concrete blocks, and the builders had not removed the evidence of their untidy stay, for there were heaps of hard mortar, a broken wheelbarrow or two, and a small stack of seasoned timber. No light showed in the house. He signalled the car to stop and, getting down, walked cautiously forward until he came to a door under a rough-cast portico. There was no bell button, but a small knocker, and he had grasped this when he felt the door yield under his slight pressure. It was open. . . .

A trap? Peter was taking no risks. From his hip pocket he drew a small Browning pistol, slipped back the jacket, and, flashing his head-lamp ahead of him, walked down the passage till he came to the right angle passage which Daphne had described. Here he stopped and listened: there was no sound.

Feeling cautiously along to the left, he came upon a black door, recessed into the wall: he recognised from Daphne's story the tiny spy-hole and, lifting it aside, peered through.

The room within was in darkness. Flashing his lamp on the door, he saw hanging on a nail, that had evidently been hastily driven into the wood, a key, and attached to the key a small luggage label. Lifting it down, he read:

'Ella Lewston, condemned to five years' penal servitude, but reprieved through a combination of circumstances.'

Remembering Daphne's description, he looked round for the light switch which controlled the lamps inside the cell, and a little way farther along the passage he found a fairly large switch-board, and in a second the whole house was illuminated.

Evidently one of the switches must have lit up the interior of the cell, for he heard the movement of a chair as he inserted the key, and then a voice screamed something unintelligible. He threw open the door.

Ella Creed was standing behind the table, staring wildly at him. She wore a coarse linen costume; her hair hung loosely over her shoulders, and he had only to see her twitching face to know the agony through which she had passed. It was a long time before he could get her sufficiently quiet to tell her story, and in her terror of the moment Ella Creed tore the last veil from the face of the Feathered Serpent. It may be produced in part from that article in the *Post-Courier* which electrified London.

XXIII

THE STORY OF THE FEATHERED SERPENT

By Peter Dewin

The incidents described above merely supply the *dénoue-ment* of the remarkable drama which has held the breath-less attention of the world during the past few days. It is my task to place in chronological order the strange and tragic causes which led to the murder of two seemingly respectable citizens, the abduction of one of the best known actresses in London, and finally to the fact that Gregory Beale, philanthropist, scientist, sociologist and explorer, is now a fugitive from justice with the police of the whole world on his trail.

Twelve years ago, London knew Mr. Gregory Beale as a man passionately interested in the life of the poor, and purely desirous of applying the enormous wealth which he had inherited from his father, to the alleviation of human suffering; as a dabbler in parlour socialism; as a brilliant speaker and a no less brilliant writer on those problems which most nearly touch the lives of our poorer and less fortunate citizens.

Gregory Beale was an idealist; a man who believed that with a little human effort and the expenditure of money, the ugliest spots of society could be made sweet, and her wounds healed. He was happiest only when, under one assumed name or another, he was living in slumland, giving, unknown to them, help to his poorer neighbours, and striving to solve what to him was the baffling problem of poverty. It seems incredible, but it is indubitably true, that Mr. Beale spent enormous sums of money in the East and South-east End, without those whom he benefited being aware of his identity. In conjunction with the late Mr. Walber, the well-known architect, he erected club-houses for boys and girls, recreation-rooms, even an experimental block of flats. He had it in his mind to erect the perfect tenement, when a terrible fate overtook him.

It was not to be expected that the presence of this Haroun al-Raschid in the East End of London, and the constantly occurring benefactions bestowed by some unknown millionaire, should escape the attention either of the Press or of the local people.

The Press, in its desire for news, made every effort to identify the unknown philanthropist; but their investigations were brought to naught by the fact that, warned by a previous experience, where the donation of a dock settlement house was traced to him through a cheque, Mr. Beale distributed his alms in hard cash. It was his practice to withdraw enormous sums from his bank and deposit the money in a safe deposit.

As the reader probably knows, admission to the vault of a safe deposit is only secured by the production of the key and the repeating of a password, which is adopted by the depositor when the box is rented. Mr. Beale chose the word 'Gucumatz' – that is to say, 'The Feathered Serpent.' He had taken a very deep interest in early Aztec history, and the Feathered Serpent stood for him as the symbol of creation, benevolence and loving kindness. He rented a box at the Fetter Lane Safe Deposit, in the name which he was very fond of using – William Lane. And in this box were deposited American currency bills to the value of $700,000. He intended building this enormous block of apartments – enormous, that is, for London – and it was his intention to hide his identity behind that of a mythical American millionaire.

The plans were drawn up secretly in consultation with his friend, when occurred the unthinkable tragedy which sent William Lane to a felon's cell.

In the course of his wanderings he came into contact with a man named Lewston, who afterwards called himself Leicester Crewe, and his married sister, Ella Lewston, or Farmster, the wife of a man who was convicted in the name of Farmster, who at that time owned a public-house in Tidal Basin under the name of Farmer. Farmer did not live with his wife, partly because they had quarrelled, but more by reason of the fact that, though the quarrel was made up, Lewston, whom I will call Crewe, thought it better if they pretended that they did not know one another, for at that time Crewe had conceived an ambitious project, namely the establishment of a little factory for printing forged French notes.

He laid out the whole of his capital on machinery and plant, which was smuggled into a house in the same street as that in which Joe Farmer's saloon was situated. With some difficulty, Lewston had got into touch with Paula Ricks, the daughter of the notorious forger, who was having a bad time in a little French provincial town. He brought her to England to engrave the plates, and 'business' had begun on a small scale, when Gregory Beale became acquainted with the brother and the sister.

Crewe pretended that he was a small commission agent. He lived, if not in a grand, at any rate in a comfortable and respectable style. Evidently Mr. Beale was favourably impressed, later enthusiastically, when Crewe, having been careful to discover the kind of life story Beale would like, told him a yarn of his struggles, his temptations and his small crimes. The interest grew to friendship. Beale was in the habit of calling in the evening, and he found not only an agreeable and respectful companion in Crewe, but something more in his sister. When love comes to a man of middle age, its roots sink deeply; and to the idealist Ella Creed, whose writ for libel we neither anticipate nor fear, was, in the eyes of this enamoured man, the most beautiful creature on God's earth. She was a consummate actress, sensitive to his wishes and playing the part she knew he would like best.

Exactly why Beale should be in the East End of London, they could not fathom, and he would not tell them that he was the unknown philanthropist. They guessed that he was a man with some little money, and, as Ella Creed told me last night, they decided that he might be a useful 'cover' for them in their forthcoming operations. 'We thought,' she said, 'that we might pass the buck to him if things got a little too warm.' They never dreamt that he was a millionaire, but looked upon him as a 'sucker,' as Miss Creed called him, who might be put in to take any blame or receive any punishment that was coming their way.

They were already deeply involved in Joe Farmer's nefarious sideline, for he was a conscienceless receiver of stolen property, and used his public-house mainly for that purpose. Thousands of pounds' worth of property have passed across that zinc counter. Jewel thieves from the west, opium smugglers, they were all meat to Joe Farmer, who had at this time assisting him a man called Harry Merstham, or, as he was known locally, Harry the Barman, who was probably privy to Farmer's nefarious business.

Harry the Barman had met Mr. Beale under one of his aliases, and had been a beneficiary of his; but since

Gregory Beale did not enter public-houses, it is unlikely that Harry would have ever seen the philanthropist but for subsequent happenings.

The forgery scheme was now in a fair way to being realised. Paula Ricks had arrived in England and had already made one or two remarkable engravings. The printing press was installed in a small house, and the first batch of bills was run off, though they were not circulated.

Beale's visits to Crewe and his sister became more frequent, and one night, when he was alone with the girl, this infatuated man declared his love and asked her to marry him. She was not very much astonished, but she was apparently amused; told him that she must consult her brother, and put him off for twenty-four hours. Marriage, of course, was impossible: she was already married to Farmer; but Crewe thought it would be an excellent idea if she kept her eccentric lover on a string. 'Billy said he might be very useful, and it wasn't the time to get rid of him, and that I had better accept him, and so I agreed. He used to talk a lot of stuff about our devoting our lives to the uplifting of the submerged poor, and of course I agreed with him. I never dreamt he was anything in particular, though I was sure he had more money than my brother believed he had.'

The curious thing is that he never revealed himself as Gregory, retaining his pseudonym of William Lane. Then one evening, when he called and they were alone together in the little parlour, he told her of his plan to build in that very district a great model dwelling. She treated this as idle raving, and even when he said he had the money to buy the site and commence operations immediately, she thought that was no more than a boast to impress her with his wealth.

Crewe, who had been to see the forgery plant, came

in at that moment and was let into the secret. To Ella's astonishment, he seemed impressed. 'I thought he was pulling a bluff,' said Creed in her statement to me, 'but after we'd got rid of Lane, he told me he believed there was a lot of truth in the statement. He said he thought this man might be the mysterious millionaire that everybody had been talking about, and who was known to be operating in the East End of London. He asked me to get some further particulars from Lane, and I promised.

'The next night Lane called, I told him that I was ready to be married at once. He was overjoyed, and promised me a wonderful honeymoon on the Continent before we returned to take up our work amongst the poor. I thought he was a little mad, and then he told me more about the building, and said that he had seven hundred thousand dollars at the Fetter Lane Safe Deposit. He showed me the key and told me the password.'

Apparently Ella rallied him on this, and showed a gentle scepticism. It was then that Beale committed an act of lunacy. He wrote on a sheet of paper: 'Please allow bearer to go to my box, No. 741, at any time.' Ella went, saw the money and came back with a report. Joe Farmer was called into consultation, and between the three they hatched perhaps the most diabolical plot which human ingenuity could conceive.

Already Paula Ricks was weakening. She was afraid her presence in London was known. More than this, she was not satisfied with the printing of the notes, and wanted to bring over two Frenchmen. The plot was to involve Lane in the forgery, grab the money and skip out, leaving him to bear the brunt; and as a preliminary to this, Crewe persuaded the philanthropist to go into Farmer's saloon and change a £5 note. He had a great repugnance to entering public-houses, but the excuse which Crewe offered was so plausible that he carried the note to the barman, who changed the money. The consternation of the gang, when they discovered that Harry knew who Lane was, was only equalled by their panic that he might testify that the note tendered was a genuine one. Afterwards, when Farmer reported to the police, a forged note was substituted.

Harry had already applied for a loan to go to South America, from Farmer, and this was their opportunity. Harry was shipped off on the day William Lane was married to Ella. The marriage took place in a registrar's office in East Ham, and the bridegroom, strangely enough, gave his real name, though nobody seems to have noticed the fact.

It was Ella who took her new husband to the little house where the forging plant was stowed away in a coal-house. Her position was a very delicate one, but she was, as I have already said, a consummate actress. As the hour drew near for the police raid, she told him an astonishing story, playing upon his feelings to such an extent that when the raid was made, he implicitly believed that she was the helpless victim of an unscrupulous brother, that she had forged the plates and worked the printing machines, and that she alone would suffer. 'When I told him,' said Ella, 'he was like a man stunned. He made me repeat the yarn again, and I told him that my brother and I had been carrying out these forgeries for years, and that I thought the game was nearly up. When I left him, as I did, on the pretence of going to book a new railway ticket to the Continent by way of Flushing, he was like a man in a dream.'

Before that dream could pass, the police arrived. William Lane, taking, as he thought, the burden from his wife, secure in his anonymity, and perhaps animated a little by his insatiable curiosity, was sent to penal servitude. The police made every effort to unveil his identity, but they did not succeed. On the day he was sent to prison, and not until then, Joe Farmer went to the Safe Deposit armed with the letter of authorisation, and removed the 700,000 dollars. The intention was to divide this into three parts, but an unexpected factor in Paula Ricks appeared on the scene. Very foolishly they had not kept their plot secret from her, and she claimed, and eventually received, her fourth share.

The life of William Lane in prison can only be described as one long martyrdom, and it is possible to conceive that, through the days and months he spent in a prison cell, there grew a desire for vengeance, as slowly he began to realise that he had been a dupe. Prisoners talk freely; he had not been in Dartmoor six months before he learnt that Ella was the wife of Joe Farmer, and could guess the rest.

Once he said that prison would turn the best man into a beast, and doubtless he was thinking of himself, recalling the long nights of horror, when he lay thinking, thinking, thinking . . . planning this vengeance and the other. It is certain that the William Lane who came out of prison was altogether a different being from the William Lane who went in. Whilst he was in prison his house was run as usual – his lawyer had standing instructions to carry on during his not unusual disappearances from town.

I am positive that only one outsider was in his confidence, and that was his butler, who had been in his service from childhood. There is no proof here, but the fact that the butler has disappeared leads me to believe that he was not only privy to his master's deeds, but that he was an active participant, and it is possible that he was the man who later kidnapped a young lady under the impression that he was taking

Ella Creed to the 'prison' near Epping. There is a
likelihood that Beale was in the habit of smuggling
letters out of prison to this man.

Beale planned that as soon as he came out of prison
he would slip off to America quietly, and make an
ostentatious return. Most people thought he was in
Central America, and the fact that the butler was
responsible for the circulation of the story makes me
believe that he knew the plight in which his master had
fallen.

Unfortunately for Beale's plan, two parasites, one
named Hugg, a fairly inoffensive person, and Harry the
Lag, a bullying brute who had been sentenced to a long
term of imprisonment for a wicked assault and robbery,
were released from Dartmoor on the same day; and Harry,
believing that Lane was a man of property, never let him
out of his sight until, in the neighbourhood of Thatcham, a
motor-car, driven by the owner of a house which Hugg and
Harry had burgled, killed the old lag, injured Hugg and
gave Beale his opportunity to escape.

He disappeared, returning little more than a week
ago, bringing with him curios which he said he had dug
up from ruined Aztec cities, but the majority of which,
as I learnt very early on, were part of the sale by the late
Mr. Saul Zimmerman, who was an ardent collector of
such things. Unfortunately, Beale had forgotten to remove the red sale labels, one of which came into my
possession.

Before his return – and here the butler is implicated still
further – this man had purchased a taxicab, and had
obtained a licence, and there is little doubt that, in the
guise of a taxi-man and with a small moustache resem-
bling what he wore when in prison, Beale roamed about
London looking for his enemies. It is possible that they
were located before his arrival. At any rate, his first victim

was Joe Farmer, whose false testimony had alone been responsible for sending him to prison.

The killing of Leicester Crewe was, perhaps, the most ingenious murder that has ever been perpetrated. It is certain that, on one pretext or another, Beale intended to bring Crewe to his house, and had carefully rehearsed the procedure. Crewe saved him the trouble of inventing a subterfuge: he came voluntarily two nights ago to sell some shares, and Gregory Beale was prepared for him. He had had splinter-proof glass put into his windows, and he carried into the study a steel-sheeted door to act as a target and to receive the bullet that he intended firing through the glass. Incidentally, he left a spent automatic shell in the garden to give verisimilitude to the story.

At the moment of the killing he arranged that his lawyer, Superintendent Clarke of Scotland Yard and myself should be present in the house. The crime is very easily reconstructed. He admitted Crewe into the dark passage, walked before him into the study, and, as the man came in and at the place he desired him to be, he shot him dead with a Deloraine air pistol, using a bullet which he himself had fashioned from a gold signet ring. 'It was my wedding ring,' said Ella Creed. 'We were married in such a hurry that he hadn't time to get a proper one, so he took that off his little finger and put it on mine.' Not only had Beale made this preparation, but in the dark he had chipped away the glass from the top of the wall, thrown sacks across the top, and had even made footmarks to lead the police astray.

The door was used to catch the bullet he fired through the glass and to prevent damage to the wall and stop the possibility of detection. He had designed death for the man, imprisonment for the woman, and to this latter end had bought what was originally the beginnings of a small war factory, which was never completed. As factories go, it was a tiny place, but after it came into his possession he had it fitted so that one of the rooms was a miniature cell. Undoubtedly he intended that his revenge should take that shape, and that the woman who had deceived him and sent him to a living grave should herself taste the rigours of imprisonment.

On the day of Crewe's murder, Ella Creed called at his house, and whilst examining a clay serpent, she heard his voice, recognised it, and fell into a faint. What afterwards transpired may be set down in her own words. 'I told him I'd recognised him, and he asked me to keep the matter to myself until the morrow, and he would give me a very large sum of money. I asked him if he'd killed Farmer, and he admitted he had. I threatened to inform the police, and he told me that if I did I must confess to how I got my money. He asked me to think it over and see him in the morning.'

As I have said, at the present moment Gregory Beale and his butler are fugitives from justice, and are being searched for in every direction. That Beale will be caught, I very much doubt. He is a man who for a number of years has deliberately educated himself in criminal methods, and has harnessed his undoubted genius to the evasion of punishment. Will this perfect criminal, with his knowledge of languages, his extraordinary aptitude for disguise, with a nimble mind foreseeing all possibilities, ever fall into the hands of justice? I permit myself to doubt the possibility.

'What I should like to know is,' said Clarke, 'what scared Beale? How did he know that you had got the story at your finger-tips?'

Peter's answer did not enlighten him; almost as unsatisfactory was his explanation to Daphne Olroyd, as they sat one sunny winter afternoon on the Park, her hand in his.

'But,' she insisted, 'did Mr. Beale ever ask you not to tell about him?'

'He asked me nothing,' said Peter cheerfully, 'except that he suggested I should go and have a long sleep – and I did! And whilst I slept, lo! the Feathered Serpent vanished from the land!'

THE END